8B 8128.50

S0-EGQ-040

TARGET: U.S.S. FORRESTAL

"If the balloon goes up," said Kolnikov grimly, "you'll see the biggest Fourth of July show around this ship you've ever seen in your life."

"Then what are her chances?" asked Lowell.

"Of getting off the full strike? Maybe fifty-fifty. Of surviving more than half an hour, next to zilch."

"You forgot one thing, Victor," interrupted Gruber. "If they have people *inside*, they don't need to come after us. They could simply foul up the arming of the nukes and we'd send off the whole strike armed with a hundred duds. That would allow them to concentrate their whole defense on stopping whatever's coming at them from the land."

"Yes, Max. And that would mean we couldn't break up their formations if they do invade Turkey."

"What about the Turkish army?"

"They could only delay a full-scale Soviet thrust; they're outnumbered, outgunned, outtanked. They couldn't hold more'n three days at the most before the other side flattened them."

"Christ! Then, we're it!"

"We're it, Max."

Also by Roy W. West:

CODE NAME: MOBY DICK

DESTROYER

Roy W. West

LEISURE BOOKS  NEW YORK CITY

A LEISURE BOOK

Published by

Dorchester Publishing Co., Inc.
6 East 39th Street
New York, NY 10016

Copyright ©1985 by Roy W. West

All rights reserved. No part of this book may be reproduced
or transmitted in any form or by any electronic or mechan-
ical means, including photocopying, recording or by any information storage and retrieval system, without the written
permission of the Publisher, except where permitted by law.

Printed in the United States of America

ONE

VICTOR KOLNIKOV glowered darkly through the large, plain window of the Commandant's office. Outside, the North Atlantic returned his mood in kind. The first day of spring was being icily ignored by the prevailing climate of Portsmouth, New Hampshire. Both sky and sea seemed determined to match the dirty granite walls of the Naval Prison, which loomed beside the bay like the gray hulk of a beached battleship. Patches of scudding rain raced each other westward across the wind-rippled harbor toward the mouth of the Piscataqua River. As Kolnikov watched, a four-engine jet bomber dropped out of the solid overcast and slanted noiselessly down toward the Air Force base south of the city. Kolnikov followed its progress from slat to slat across the venetian blind until it finally disappeared in a banking turn beyond Portsmouth's clustered church spires. Then he spoke without turning.

"I want my honor back, Simon . . . my honor and my commission." The flat tone of his voice was belied by his huge fists, clenched white with stony determination.

The tall, aristocratic man seated on the red leather couch across the room shifted his too-long legs to yet another uncomfortable position. He wore the dress blue uniform of a Captain in the United States Navy. The four gold stripes and Line star on his sleeve caught the light from the ornate brass table lamp as he removed his cigarette to reply.

"If this works, Victor, you'll have both— I promise you."

Kolnikov still did not turn. His unruly hair, once coal black but mostly gray now, reflected the dismal scene outside. He stared straight ahead as if searching for a second plane. His lips barely moved now as he spoke through gritted teeth.

"Where's Gelman?"

"He's not your concern," replied the Captain with quietly emphatic finality. "Not now."

Kolnikov wheeled around to confront his companion in the impressively decorated room; the force of his turn ruffled an American flag which stood between himself and an expansive oak desk.

"Not my concern?" he growled. "Not my concern? Nine years in this goddamn hole . . . my commission, my honor, my mother and father . . . not my concern, you say?" Kolnikov's face had turned livid; it worked crazily atop his powerful body. Tears crept out furtively from under the heavy eyelids beneath scowling, shaggy black brows suggesting Eastern European peasant stock. "Gelman is my only concern . . . now. That Jew-bastard put me in here; he framed us all —you know that, Simon. He killed my parents. And I'm going to get him if it's the last thing I ever do on this earth."

The other man sprang up from the sofa and bounded over to face down squarely at

Kolnikov; though probably of the same weight, he stood more than a head taller.

"You're not going to get Gelman or anybody else!" he commanded. The shorter man did not budge, but relaxed slightly as if grudgingly deferring to the other's authority. "And if you don't agree to my terms—and that means you do nothing but exactly what I tell you, especially about Gelman—you won't get out of here until they send your remains to your next of kin!"

Kolnikov stood his ground and slowly surveyed the Captain from head to toe as if contrasting his own faded blue prison dungarees with the other's nautical elegance. His gaze returned momentarily to the gold stripes, then straight up to the tall man's eyes.

"You know, Simon, I'd probably be a Captain now, except for Gelman and his two buddies. That's another one I owe him."

The tall man turned on his heel and paced away down the room, speaking as he went. "You'll get that, too, Victor . . . or you probably will . . . but only if you let me run the show my way." He stopped, then turned to face Kolnikov. "I want Gelman too . . . almost as badly as you do. Why do you think I set this up?" He gestured with his hands; his voice was pleading now. He took a deep breath and continued. "Victor, I'm going out on the yardarm for you—literally. If this blows up in our faces, you'll have another cellmate—*me!*"

Both men grimaced at the thought. The Captain continued. "That's why you've got to play it my way—all the way."

"I want Gelman and his gang dead," Kolnikov interjected; he unclenched his hands and thrust them roughly into his pockets. The tall one strode up to Kolnikov and punctuated his words with a finger thrusting into the middle of Kolnikov's massive chest. He shouted.

"Stop talking like a pig-headed *kulak* . . ." Kolnikov's glare arrested him. "I . . . I'm sorry, Victor, I didn't mean it *that* way . . . What I mean to say is . . . I want Gelman . . . yes . . . but I want you vindicated as well . . . and Gruber and Lowell . . . and we can't do that if you go off on a personal vendetta."

"What *about* Gruber and Lowell?"

"They've agreed. But it won't work without you; it's either all three or we scrap the whole thing."

Kolnikov turned back to the window.

"Let me think about it."

The Captain walked back to the couch, sat down, and lit up another cigarette. He regarded Kolnikov warily through the curling smoke.

Captain Simon Alexander Roschestvensky, USN—born Simeone Alexandrovitch—was the third and last child of Alexander and Ludmilla Roschestvensky and a great grandnephew of the Admiral who bungled the Russian Asiatic Fleet into total defeat at the hands of Admiral Togo at the Battle of Tsushima Strait in 1905, a disaster that triggered Imperial Russia's final slide from its position as a world power and presaged the even greater disasters which were to befall her nine years later. Under that cloud already, the Roschestvenskys were among the first to perceive the logic of decamping ahead of the Bolsheviks. Unlike the brilliant Admiral Makarov, whose uncharacteristic consideration for the common men under him is even now honored by the Soviet state, Roschestvensky bequeathed his heirs a legacy of official hatred. Making their way across Siberia ahead of the defeated and retreating White Admiral Kolchak, the Roschestvenskys melted in with the thousands of stateless nobles who flowed through the Shanghai Bund to uncertain exile. They reached San Francisco, and Simon was born there just twelve years after the family debarked tired and penniless in 1922. The modest house in which he grew up was ever compared longingly, especially by their mother, with the Roschestvensky palace on St. Petersburg's ultra-exclusive Nevsky Prospekt overlooking the Neva.

A brilliant, precocious child from the start, Simon was an excellent student and an easy candidate for a full scholarship to prestigious American University. There he studied International Affairs and Political Science, and there he met his fellow classmate and future colleague—also on scholarship—Victor Kolnikov. Though never close friends—due in large part to their different social backgrounds—they had entered the Navy, and eventually Naval Intelligence, together, moving up almost in parallel in the shadow world of Counter Intelligence. Two things they did share: a talent for Byzantine intrigue which seems native to all Russians, aristocrat and peasant alike, and a certain nagging distrust for the traditionally WASP Intelligence Establishment—though Roschestvensky enjoyed a distinct advantage because of his aristocratic heritage. They were both better off, however, than Arnold Gelman, only son of a German Jewish university professor and his wife, fugitives from Nazi Germany. Gelman was roundly detested by everybody as a Jew. And the incontestable genius which drove him forward fanned the flames of hatred.

Physically, Roschestvensky and Kolnikov could not have been less alike. With a beard, Simon would have made a picture-book Czar; Kolnikov looked like a peasant.

Roschestvensky regretted his slip of the tongue with Victor. But even in democratic America, the ancient, underlying prejudices found voice now and then.

Finally, Kolnikov broke the silence.

"Where will Gruber and Lowell be?"

"They'll be located elsewhere. And you're not to try to contact them." Simon was reading Kolnikov's mind, if not his eyes. "Besides, they'll be under very deep cover, with aliases you won't be able to trace."

"Then how will Gelman find us?" Kolnikov was getting interested for the first time. Roschestvensky relaxed slightly; he let out a sigh.

"Only someone with access to the files will know where you are—or even that you're out. And for the last time, Victor, we're not certain it's Gelman—or ever was. You were monitoring others as well; you know that."

10

Kolnikov nodded reluctantly. Roschestvensky chain-lit another cigarette; he continued. "Whoever the mole is—or are—they're deep, very deep . . . at least fifteen years. And for that matter, somebody else, a lot higher up . . . maybe even in another agency . . . could be controlling the whole thing—which would account for their not getting caught by now." Roschestvensky shrugged. "We simply don't know."

Kolnikov moved over and rested his bottom against the edge of the desk facing Roschestvensky. He waved his right hand emphatically.

"Christ, Simon! You've had enough time. At least nine years." He lapsed into silence; the other took up the thread.

"That's what has us all baffled—and worried. There's been nothing, absolutely nothing, for nine years; not since you three were blown away." Roschestvensky watched Kolnikov's eyes for a reaction as he played his next card. "This means one of two things, Victor: either they're building up to something really big, or you were guilty."

Kolnikov exploded. "Goddamn! *Goddamn,* Simon. I'm not guilty, and neither are Gruber and Lowell. You know it . . . you knew it at the time—you were the only one of those chicken bastard *friends* of ours who stood up for us at the court-martial!"

Roschestvensky nodded, then shook his head. "Yes, I did stand up for you—on faith. But I still don't *know.* Only you three and God know for certain—and whoever set you up, if they did."

11

Kolnikov spat. "Then, you're saying even you think we could be guilty!" Suddenly his scowl shifted to a look of theatrical cunning. "But, then . . . you wouldn't be doing this if you really thought that. Would you?"

Roschestvensky smiled, then grew serious. "That's basically it. We don't have a single lead. Gelman—everybody's been clean as a whistle ever since you three went in."

"And we're your last card," offered Kolnikov, leaping ahead. "And you think if you spring us, it'll shake something loose . . . make them think we're all on to something . . . and *they'll* come out like the curious fox, huh?"

"Exactly, Victor. Whoever it was wanted you safely out of the way for a long time . . . for good, as it's turned out . . . or so they think. But after nine years and *nothing* . . ." Roschestvensky stubbed out his cigarette and spread his hands. "And frankly, I'm worried. Taking this much time . . . without a single move . . . has to be for something so big . . . so devastating . . . it makes my flesh creep."

"And what makes you want to smoke them out now, at this specific time?"

"I can feel something coming, Victor." Roschestvensky was sitting foward now, his hands flattened together between his knees. He instinctively lowered his voice. "Don't ask me why . . . but lately . . . call it instinct, call it nearly twenty years' experience . . . call it what you will . . . I just sense that something's about to go down. Certainly, the time's ripe

. . . the whole Middle East mess heated up and shifting almost every day: first Iran, then Afghanistan. Tito's gone . . . it's the 1914 Balkan Powder Keg all over again . . . it could start anywhere." He shook his head and sat back, his eyes closed.

"And you want to bring us out as decoys . . . uh . . . to throw a monkey wrench in their timetable, right?"

Kolnikov walked across to the couch and stood over Roschestvensky, who looked up at him.

"Yes, Victor. It's my last card, my only card. You'll be in such deep cover that only a mole could find you—or know—or care. And if they move on you, they're blown."

"But why move on us at all?"

"If something really big's about to go down soon, and you three come out at just this moment, they'll *have* to find out what's up— and then I've got 'em and their big game gets cancelled. And that's why you can't go off on your own." Roschestvensky paused to let Kolnikov mull over his words.

"Are you in, Victor?"

"Do I have a choice?"

"None at all—unless you want to stay here."

Kolnikov shrugged. "Then I'll do it . . . for a while . . . but, if it doesn't work, Simon, I'm going to take out Gelman myself . . . and Horn . . . and Stoddard . . ."

Roschestvensky stood up and clasped Kolnikov's left forearm. He spoke calmly, like a sentencing judge.

"Then I'd have to stop you."

"You'll have to kill me."

Roschestvensky nodded. "That too. I hope you don't make me do it."

"Then you better be right, Simon, because you'll never get me back in here alive."

"I know that too. But we'll cross that bridge when we come to it. Now will you do it —exactly my way?"

Kolnikov grinned broadly.

"Simon, I'd suck cock to get out of this place after nine years. Of course I'll play it your way. At least until it looks as if your way isn't working."

Roschestvensky brightened and clasped Kolnikov's hand tightly.

"Good. Now let's get this thing underway."

Roschestvensky turned to leave. Kolnikov reached out and pulled him back. He grasped the tall man's right hand with both of his.

"Thank you, Simon . . . I . . ."

The tears had crept back into his eyes.

TWO

Two HOURS later, Kolnikov was on a Greyhound bus speeding south along the coast out of Portsmouth. He had exchanged his dungarees for a cheap, gray worsted suit of indifferent fit, a plain white regulation shirt, and a tie of dubious status. His few other possessions reposed in a medium-sized kit bag on the empty aisle seat beside him.

Though he could have caught a last glimpse of the prison across the water, he didn't look back. Instead, he fished a soiled, dog-eared piece of paper out of his left coat pocket. Kolnikov unfolded it for what must have been the thousandth time, judging from the tattering of its creases. He had owned it for years, since even before his trial and imprisonment; he had torn it from a magazine while serving a boring tour of duty aboard the supercarrier *Forrestal*. It was his favorite cartoon. It had amused him then. It had often conforted him during the long years in prison. And now it especially amused him.

It pictured two men chained hand and foot, spreadeagled on the wall on a dungeon, and the one on the left was saying to the one on the right, "Now here's my plan."

Kolnikov's face crinkled up like the paper he held. He chuckled to himself.

Because he, Victor Kolnikov, had a plan.

15

And it wasn't Roschestvensky's, it didn't involve him. Nor Gelman, for that matter, nor even Naval Intelligence.

He refolded the paper and replaced it in its hiding place. Then he turned to contemplate the first landscape he had seen in nearly a decade.

Men sent to military prison for grave offenses usually end up as one of two diametrically opposed types. They either become superpatriotic, like the Man Without A Country, building pitiful shrines to the lost nation they now love desperately, as some men pine for the lost love of a woman, or they become bitter and revengeful. Kolnikov was one of the latter. He was bitter, very bitter.

But, unlike those who simply lash out in their fury, Kolnikov had a plan to avenge the injustice, the hurt he felt was done him by a stupid government and service. Not that it involved any real harm to his country; that wasn't his style. Victor Kolnikov merely planned to get rich—immensely rich—in a way which would acutely embarrass the Naval Establishment. Especially his colleagues in Naval Intelligence who had so cravenly thrown him to the wolves those many years ago.

His only regret was for Simon Roschestvensky. Simon, who alone stood by him when everyone else was howling for his blood, through the torture of nine years' frustrated innocence, and who, even now, was trusting him for one last, desperate throw of the dice.

Kolnikov felt like a shit for doing this to Simon. Still, he couldn't help but congratulate himself on the morning's performance. Masterful. Absolutely masterful! Now, when he made his move, Simon and everybody else would be looking toward Gelman and Washington while he struck elsewhere, and in a manner none of them could possibly guess. Even Gruber and Lowell—integral parts of his plan—hadn't the slightest inkling of Victor's true intent. They'd be told in good time.

For now, Kolnikov was content to take in the sights of freedom, dull and soggy as they were.

Until now, Victor Joseph Kolnikov had never perpetrated a criminal act. That is, if you don't count murdering enemy agents and traitors in the line of duty. And until Gelman framed him, his duty had been ferreting out —and occasionally taking out—the other side's agents, with emphasis on "moles," long-term plants in the U.S. intelligence establishments.

Born on the other end of the social scale from his university classmate, Kolnikov had nevertheless won Roschestvensky's respect and trust, if only because he overachieved in everything he did. Even in football—in Manayunk, everybody played football. There was even a nice ethnic division of labor there: the Italian kids quarterbacked and ran and the Poles and Ukrainians blocked and tackled, an invincible combination. And he excelled in scholarship. The combination had gotten him a better education that his parents' hardest labors could have bought. A cum-laude graduate in Slavic History and

Languages—he spoke all the major ones like a native—he was targeted by the Intelligence Establishment early in his junior year. He chose the Navy for the same basic reason as Roschestvensky: it was the prestige service.

Yes, he had come a long way from the little stone row house in Philadelphia's working-class Manayunk section, the son of Ukrainian immigrant parents and born at the height of the Great Depression.

A long way up. And a long way down.

Now, he was ex-Lieutenant Commander Kolnikov. Ex-officer. Ex-gentleman. A convicted traitor in the eyes of his family, neighbors, and country. And not even a parolee now, but out on the shortest of leashes, as bait—bait which hopefully might just flush out the real culprits and clear his name.

His name! It meant nothing to him anymore. The only two others who mattered were dead. Fuck his name! He would settle now for money. Money and revenge.

But he was free. Something he had begun to despair of. The words of the president of the court-martial were hard to forget: "...for the rest of your natural life." And in the services—particularly on an Intelligence rap—that meant nothing less than life. They had even kept one small section of that stinking prison open just for the three of them. Seven years. With a "commandant" and a skeleton crew and a few cells just for them, as if they were a bacillus of treason which could infect the other felons.

Kolnikov mouthed a crude Ukrainian blasphemy.

But now. Now a plan. A plan he had hatched years ago, a plan he had devised and embellished more to assuage the boredom of prison life than anything else, had suddenly been made possible. And he was going to carry it out. In fact, his mind had kicked it into high gear almost from the moment Roschestvensky had surprised him that morning with his offer of conditional release.

And the hell with Roschestvensky's plan. Not that Kolnikov didn't crave vindication— or had once, almost pathetically. Until his mother died.

No. There was a hitch in Roschestvensky's plan: it might not work. In which case, he— Kolnikov—would go back for the rest of his life at hard labor. And he was having none of that. He was getting out. For good.

And rich!

And fuck the vindication!

THREE

THE BUS nosed into Boston's St. James Street Terminal right on time. Kolnikov took out the railroad timetable Roschestvensky had given him and doublechecked. He had a half hour to make his train at Back Bay Station right off Copley Square, less than three blocks away. An easy walk.

Detouring slightly to the Square itself, Kolnikov headed for the ornate bar of the baroque Copley Plaza Hotel, which dominates the Square's south side. He took his time surveying the cornucopia of brands lining the back wall of the bar until his eyes settled on one which proclaimed its contents as Vodka Stolichnaya, Russia's finest—one hundred proof. Victor told the waiting bartender to pour him a double on the rocks with a cut of lime and a little soda on the side. When it arrived, he held the glass up in his big, hairy paw like some ancient Slavic conqueror inspecting some strange and exotic jewel. He sipped it. Savored it. Then drank it down in one slow, luxurious quaff.

He got the bartender's eye again.

"Give me another double. No . . . make it two doubles. Set 'em up next to each other, right here."

Then he walked off to a door marked "Gentlemen," returned shortly to finish both drinks in quick succession, paid his tab, and headed back out through the lobby.

The national drink of his forefathers had already banished much of the dank New England winter. The first good stuff in nine years! One of many things that'd taste good again.

Before leaving the lobby, he stopped by the telephone booths, which also hosted a bank of out-of-town directories. He selected the Manhattan book. Under V, he found it: "Vivaldi, M.C.," with address and number. He committed both to memory, and arrived at the station with five minutes to spare.

Once aboard the train, he located the bar car and startled the attendant with an order for six vodkas on the rocks—one every ten minutes, after which, he explained, he'd slow down to one every twenty until they reached New York.

But for all his ursine bulk, Kolnikov was feeling the unaccustomed alcohol by the time the train broke into the open countryside. The late afternoon sun was under the western edge of the clouds now, its rays making the landscape twinkle gold between the patches of shower. It was exactly the color of Victor Kolnikov's dream. And he toasted it with his fourth—or was it fifth?—vodka before lapsing into a deep, untroubled sleep.

The copy of that day's *New York Times* still lay in his lap unread when they crossed Hell Gate Bridge nearly six hours later.

FOUR

THE TRAIN pulled into Penn Station a predictable half hour late, having deferred right-of-way to a fast freight somewhere up in Connecticut. Kolnikov retrieved his bag from the overhead rack and passed swiftly up to the street level, where he slipped into a waiting cab. Obedient to Roschestvensky's instructions, he directed the driver straight to a hotel on Eighth Avenue about twenty blocks north from the station. From the address, Kolnikov figured it for a flea bag.

As soon as they cleared the taxi ramp, Kolnikov repositioned himself to see easily out the rear window and, ignoring the cabbie's chatter, watched for a tail. There was none; and when they neared an outdoor telephone booth just below Forty-seventh Street, Kolnikov ordered the driver over to the curb.

Moving quickly and keeping one eye down the avenue, he dialed the number he had memorized in Boston. A husky female voice answered. Kolnikov's face came alive.

"Tina Vivaldi?"

"Yes?"

"It's Victor Kolnikov."

"Victor?" She paused for what seemed minutes, then fairly screamed into the receiver. "*Darling!*" Victor winced. She had that habit of certain New York women of drawling out an h before the r. She paused again, as if trying to digest an incredible idea. Then out tumbled a flood.

"Victor, darling . . . what? . . . I . . . what are you doing in . . . I mean, when did you get out . . . I thought . . ."

Kolnikov, nodding vigorously, interrupted her in midsentence.

"Calm down, Tina . . . please. Yes, it's me . . . but I can't talk here . . . or now . . ."

"But I thought you'd never . . ."

"Tina, will you *please* shut up!" There was silence. Victor began urgently. His eyes kept flitting up and down the street. "Tina, I want to see you in . . . say, about an hour. Are you free?"

"Is this business or personal?" The voice was calmer, though still excited.

"Strictly personal."

"In that case, you know I'm always free to you, darling."

"I'll be there as fast as I can."

"But, Victor, how . . ."

"I'll tell you everything when I get there." Kolnikov puckered a loud kiss into the mouthpiece and hung up on the still-babbling Tina, then hurried back into the cab. He looked at his watch; just nine-thirty-four. If he was being timed, he'd still arrive at the hotel clean. He sat back and fished a cigarette out of a nearly empty pack.

FIVE

THE HOTEL, so-called, was an even worse flea bag than Victor had feared. Cheap bastards, he thought to himself as he paid off the taxi and strode up the two badly worn steps to a narrow, underlighted pretense for a lobby.

The Puerto Rican room clerk who arrived after the fourth or fifth ring of the bell was surly and indifferent. He didn't acknowledge Kolnikov's having a reservation, something certainly as rare as virginity in the broads who were openly appraising him from just inside the doorway.

The elevator was unmanned and excruciatingly slow. When it finally disgorged him with a jolt and a clatter, Kolnikov felt he should have been on the fortieth floor instead of only the fourth. His room was as frayed as the hall carpet, and as dirty. Christ! he thought, can they afford it?

Twenty minutes later, he was back on the street, shaved and perked up as best he could in his crummy bathroom. The accommodations at Portsmouth were bigger and a helluva lot cleaner. He made a mental note to thank Navel Intelligence for their generosity at the first possible occasion.

Ignoring the street hookers—and the boys that took up the call when the girls failed— Kolnikov strolled south for three blocks until he spied a likely bar and wandered warily in. A floozie blonde arrived at the same time as his watered scotch.

"Hi, honey. Got a light?"

Kolnikov took indifferent note of her breasts, jacked up until they overflowed the cheap purple gown, which somehow obscenely complemented the bleached-out yellow of her hair.

"How much?"

"How much for what?"

"How much for a trick?"

"Hey, buster . . . what kinda person you think I am, anyway?"

"I *know* what sort of person you are. Now, how much for a trick?"

"You a cop?"

"No."

"Fifty dollars, if that's the way y'er gonna be." The tart made an unconvincing face of hurt innocence.

"Okay. Let's go." Kolnikov bolted his drink and stood up toward the entrance, his back to the girl. She reached up to his shoulder and tugged.

"Hey, honey," she whined, "aren't y' gonna buy me a lousy drink?"

"No. Now do you want the job or don't you? If you don't . . ."

"All right. All right! I'm coming . . . creep."

Kolnikov hustled her outside.

"Where's your place?"

"Over on Ninth Avenue. We can walk."

"We'll take a cab."

"But I said . . ."

"*I* said we'll take a cab."

The girl shot an appraising glance at Kolnikov's cheap suit.

"Okay, buster, it's your money . . . and by the way, you didn't tell me your name."

"You can call me John—okay?"

The hooker lapsed into a sullen pout as they settled into the back seat of the taxi. Kolnikov told the driver to head west at the next cross street. As they descended toward the even sleezier block, he turned to the sulking girl.

"How much for all night?"

"Two hundred—cash—in advance."

Kolnikov ordered the driver to pull over. He pulled the envelope containing the money Roschestvensky had given him in Portsmouth from his inside coat pocket. He counted off fifteen twenties and closed them up in the startled girl's hand.

"Here's *three* hundred. Now I want you to go home and stay there for the rest of the night." He pointed at the money. "That's six tricks—more than you can pick up tonight, and fifty percent more than for an all-night stand. Is it a deal?"

"What are you, fella, some sort religious nut?"

Kolnikov spun around in the seat and grasped her jaw from underneath, his giant fingers twisting her heavily rouged cheeks in against her teeth with the force of a quickly spun vise. She yelped, her eyes bulged wide with pain and fear. Kolnikov's cherubic smile counterpointed the venomous glitter of his eyes. His whisper was the hissing of a snake.

"It doesn't matter what I am. I've paid you. And now you're going to do exactly what I told you to do." Frightened tears were rolling down the girl's tortured cheeks as she glanced pleadingly toward the driver, who was studiously ignoring them both. "You're going to go home and stay there until tomorrow morning. Because, if I catch you back there tonight . . . if you take one step outside . . . or say one word . . . to anyone . . ." He paused for effect, still holding the girl rigid with terror. "If it gets back that I wasn't with you all night . . . I'll cut your throat. Or better yet, I'll tell your boss you held out a hundred dollars on him and let him do it his way."

The last statement visually hit home. Kolnikov let go of the girl, quickly passed a ten to the cabbie; then, before getting out, he turned again to the sobbing girl. She was ghastly white, even under all the pancake. Kolnikov kissed her gently.

"Okay, sweetheart. Now go home and stay there . . . like a good girl."

Then he was out the door and around the corner in a dozen quick strides.

SIX

It was nearly eleven when Kolnikov's circuitous route brought him to the Spanish Revival lobby of the yellow brick apartment house on Fifty-ninth Street near the East River. Nameless save for its prestige address, it was one of the buildings preferred by New York insiders. Even facing the Queensboro Bridge with its unceasing honk and roar—the kiss of death anywhere else—couldn't dent either its desirability or the discreet aplomb of the doorman who announced a late visitor to the occupant of 22-B.

Tina was waiting framed in the open door of her flat when Victor stepped out of the elevator. She was wrapped in a wine-red silk robe, trimmed with two inches of mink about the cuffs and collar and continuing down the front and around the floor-length hem. It was tied at the waist with a narrow sash of the same fur, and lay open nearly that far down in front. It neatly quartered a body which needed no enhancement whatsoever.

She held a double old-fashioned glass filled perilously close to the brim.

"Victor, darling! What a delightful surprise!"

Kolnikov enveloped her in his thick arms in the doorway and planted a hungry kiss on her wide, wet, full mouth. Simultaneously, he slipped a hand down and under the curve of her deliciously rounded bottom and pulled her hips hard up against his.

"Not here, Victor. You'll spill your drink. I made it just for you, with a cut of lime. Even went out to the store for your favorite. Now come inside."

Kolnikov let go of her reluctantly. She closed the door, laid the drink down on a small hall stand, then wrapped him head to toe in a sensuous embrace to the accompaniment of writhing and half-muttered endearments. Victor returned her desire with redoubled passion, while simultaneously noting—not without relief—that, save for a few enhancing character lines in the face and a bit more rounding where he most appreciated it, nine years hadn't much changed his most favorite woman in the world.

Maria Cristina Vivaldi was every man's sex dream of an Italian woman. Tall, busty, bottomy, hippy, leggy—something for everybody—with mahogany hair that tumbled and flounced like waterfalls about a classic Roman face. Her long, slender nose surmounted a full, facile mouth that vied for attention with flashing chestnut eyes. Her native intelligence needed no formal schooling. She encompassed knowledge the way she encompassed men—all at once, in *toto*, and to her best advantage. Always giving as good as she got.

Early on, she divined that her beauty, wit, and charm comprised her ticket out of the pushcart provinciality of Grand Street. And she took it. And never looked back. She was read out of the fold for transgressing the strictures of *famiglia*, home, and Church. But she didn't care. She saw it all for the soul-imprisoning swindle it was.

Of course, the deadliest sin in the world of her fathers was her attitude toward sex. Cristina Vivaldi loved the body that had freed her from the fate of Italian *moglia di casa*. She loved the pleasure that every part of it gave her, especially when a good man was inside it. In a word, Tina Vivaldi loved getting laid—voluptuously and often—but with reservations. Her men should be men of great wealth and social position, or power and influence, of beauty and talent and intelligence, and they had to be interesting both in and out of bed. In an earlier age, the French would have termed her *une grande horizontelle*.

She was perfect for certain types of Intelligence work. And that is how she came to know Victor Kolnikov.

Naval Intelligence was only one of several agencies that used Tina's lusty talents to winkle important information out of the sexually vulnerable diplomats, corporate executives, senior military officers, and foreign agents who make up so large a part of Manhattan's busy cocktail circuit. The United Nations, further south along the River, was Tina's favorite gold mine; a whole world of covert knowledge lay there, ripe for panning and refining for the good of Tina and Country.

Victor had discovered her first. It was even his idea to have the young courtesan trained as an interior decorator, a trade which pro-

vided a perfectly plausible entree almost anywhere.

And Tina literally threw herself into her
work. Early on, Victor nicknamed her Tina
Vivulva in honor of the vigor of her enormous
sexual appetite; characteristically, she
reveled in the appellation. It was also the one
secret they shared with no one else. Kolnikov
had violated the rule that a controller never
gets into bed with the controlled.

Tina also had a special thing for Russians.
The challenge of melting the uptight KGB
men who infested the Soviet delegation was
irresistible. Besides, there was that Slavic
talent for fierce, no-holds-barred fornication
which always left her, as she put it, "feeling
well-bred." Unbeknown to Victor, she had
even ensnared Roschestvensky—once. He
was very competent, but so coldly controlled
he left her feeling more frustrated than when
some growling great bear of a Slav's short
fuse left her hanging.

Victor, by comparison, combined an
honest, natural, animal lust with an incredible command of his groin. He could bring
her on in seconds and keep her there while
he drove away at her for hours. He could
wring her out and hang her up to dry, and she
loved him for it. In fact, if she ever limited
herself to only one man, that one man would
be Victor Kolnikov. Not only because he
could totally slake her desire, but because
she genuinely loved the man she called her
Russian Teddy Bear. What's more, she suspected that he loved her.

But right now her consuming desire was to

know what had brought him from that gray tomb on the Atlantic. Or how . . . or who . . .

She slipped deftly away from Kolnikov's bear hug and led him into a large, luxurious living room which she had obviously designed to frame her voluptuous person.

"Sit here, love," she cooed as she prodded Kolnikov down onto a long, L-shaped couch draped with rich, parti-colored furs and fussed a huge mushy pillow back behind his head. Victor smiled; he noted that she had dropped the phony "dahling." "Here's your drink. Now sit there a minute and relax while I get mine." She caressed his rugged cheek with the back of her soft hand and swirled away toward an array of cabinetry which divided the living room from the kitchen. Kolnikov stretched his tired bulk deeper into the soft furs.

Now, as Tina busied herself over her drinks, nine years of questions jostled each other for first place.

"When did you get out? Or have you been out for awhile?"

"Just this morning, and I came straight here." His answers raced to keep up with Tina's rapid-fire cross-examination. "No, I'm not cleared . . . I'm not on parole, not exactly . . ."

"On the run then?"

"No, not on the run."

"Then what are you on?"

"I can't say."

"Then why are you here?"

"You."

"Just me?"

"Just you."

Tina carried her drink over to the couch and perched on the edge. "How flattering, Victor. Nine years without a woman and you come straight to me." Then a scowl darkened her face. "Or did you stop along the way?"

"Not for a moment."

The darkness still held. "You're sure this isn't a professional visit?"

"Absolutely."

"But why didn't you write?"

"We weren't permitted to—to anybody. But you didn't write to me. Why not?"

"I did write you, Victor. Several times. The letters were all returned marked undeliverable."

"Bastards."

"Oh, my poor darling!" She leaned over and ran her hand gently through his hair and behind his neck. "And you're turned so gray." As she leaned to touch his far shoulder, the front of her robe gaped open, revealing two stunningly full and smooth bronzed breasts. Kolnikov reached up and ran his fingers lightly over the soft, warm flesh; he touched them gingerly, as if to prove to himself that this wasn't all a dream. Tina gave a little shiver.

"Tell me," Tina asked with a coy twinkle, "how did you manage for nine years with nothing but men to look at?"

"I didn't turn queer, if that's what you want to know." He grinned impishly. "But I've become very attracted to my right hand."

He held it up, inspected it, then kissed it with exaggerated tenderness. "We've even contemplated marriage."

Tina threw her head back and laughed in her rich contralto. "You horny devil! Did you ever think of me when you were with *her?*" She swatted his hand with an air of mock jealousy.

"Most of the time."

Tina's lewd smile parted her lips, revealing her perfect white teeth. "You haven't changed one bit!" She took Kolnikov's empty glass and glided back to the bar. He studied her underslung buttocks as they undulated across the room. His groin had been plaguing him almost continuously since he first found Tina's name in the directory. But now, after nine years, and another twelve hours, the thought of her naked under him in person seemed strangely unreal. Somehow the bed in the next room loomed alien. Victor had had Tina a thousand times squared, it seemed, or his hard cot in Portsmouth. Yet, now that she was so near in place and time, the consummation of his yearning was all strangely dreamlike. He closed his eyes. Tina's voice brought them open.

"Here, love." She thrust the fresh drink into his hand and clinked her glass against his, then spoke:

"Aqua fresca,
"Vino puro,
"Fica streta,
"Cazzo duro!"

It was their favorite toast; Tina had taught it to Victor. It wishes a man everything he

34

could want out of life—or should—at least if he's a Mediterranean. Translated literally, it says:

"Fresh water,

"Good wine,

"A tight cunt,

"A hard cock."

Victor had forgotten it, but now he repeated it back to her in Italian, toasting each line as he recited it, then adding: "I've certainly got the *cazzo duro.*"

"I know. I spotted it the moment you stepped off the elevator, and it hasn't gone down since—ah . . . *caro Vittorio mio!*"

"And what of my *vivulva?*"

"Soaking wet since you telephoned."

"Then what are we waiting for?" Victor reached for the space between Tina's tanned thighs. She wasn't lying; she was wet to the knees!

Tina sidestepped Victor's lunge for her and gamboled lightly and quickly toward the bedroom door, giggling like a lecherous schoolgirl.

Kolnikov bounded across the room after her, his groin tingling with long pent-up desire. He could feel the blood pounding in his parts; it made him stagger. Or rather, what he saw when he reached the bedroom door staggered him. He stopped dead.

Tina was sprawled already naked across a gigantic, fur-covered bed; she had shed her robe in one smooth motion as she crossed the room. But it was the room itself that stopped Kolnikov.

Every inch of wall and ceiling was covered

with natural cork. Heavy draperies hid the windows and even the closet doors above a thick turf of beige carpet. There wasn't a sound-reflective surface larger than a telephone in the whole room!

When Tina spoke, at last, it was as if they were in a soundproof chamber.

"The neighbors complained about the noise. You know I can't hold my tongue when I'm getting it." Her bare arm took in the entire room with one grand, languid sweep. "So, rather than suffer in silence—or move—I made it so they can't possibly hear me."

Kolnikov took three steps into the room and began undressing—slowly, neatly, deliberately.

"They're going to hear you tonight!"

SEVEN

THE UNNATURAL quiet of Tina's bedroom made Victor oversleep. It was already light when he paid off the taxi on Ninth Avenue and prudently walked the last five blocks to his hotel through the first stirrings of morning in New York. In this neighborhood, the sidewalks were littered with the detritus of a hundred nights before. It made him think of his head, something he would rather not do after all that booze after all those years. He tried, instead, to concentrate on his crotch, which felt much better.

Simon was waiting in Kolnikov's room; he was not entirely unexpected. His eyes were angrier than his voice.

"Where the hell have you been?"

"Out getting laid. What d'you think?"

"With whom?" Roschestvensky's eyes bore in steadily on Kolnikov.

"With some hooker from Ninth Avenue. Picked her up down the street, last night." Kolnikov casually slipped off his coat and tie, stripped to the waist, and sauntered into the bathroom.

Roschestvensky followed him and stood in the doorway.

"What's her name?"

"I don't know and I don't care. After nine years, you don't stand on formality." Kolnikov caught Simon's reflection in the greasy mirror; he was regarding the evidence of Tina's passion on Victor's savaged bare back. Kolnikov bent over the filthy basin and tried the hot-water tap; it hissed menacingly, so he settled for the cold. Then he straightened up, inspected his unshaven face, and pointed down at the impotent hot-water spigot. "Great place your boys got for me. You sure it won't bust the budget?" But Roschestvensky was not being deflected.

"You're lying, Victor!"

"About what?" Kolnikov started splashing cold water over the hungover face in the mirror.

"You were with Tina Vivaldi. That little charade with the hooker didn't work."

Kolnikov flushed slightly, but still didn't look up from his washing. "Shit! Three hundred dollars of the Navy's hard-earned money—wasted! I take it, then, you have her staked out?"

"We do. You went in at ten-fifty-three and came out at four-ten."

"Then, why ask me?"

"What did you tell her?"

Kolnikov beamed. He stood up, wet a towel, and turned his back toward the mirror as he daubed at the still-bloody scratches. Then he turned to Roschestvensky.

"If you've got her staked, you've got her wired. You know what we said . . . every god-damn word. And I hope you diddled yourself sore!"

Roschestvensky's face registered a direct hit. He had heard every word, every sound of Victor and Tina's monumental lovemaking, and the comparison with his own performance with her—and her subsequent rejection of him—was hurtful. Observing Simon, Kolnikov thought he detected jealousy in his face, and it was several seconds before the lanky aristocrat could get his mental guns trained back on Victor.

"Victor, I told you—no contacts!"

"You said no chasing Gelman. You also heard her say she isn't working for anyone anymore."

"You don't know that. She could have been part of the whole frame."

Kolnikov darkened. "I doubt it."

"That's not a very professional statement, coming from you."

"I'm not a professional anymore . . . remember? You took that away from me nine years ago too."

"But you're still under orders. And if you disobey them and blow this thing, you go back in the hole until they put you in a rubber bag . . . no vindication, no honor, no commission, no nothing—not even a name on your coffin, just a serial number. So stay away from Tina Vivaldi!"

Kolnikov tossed the towel in the sink and stepped over to Simon. The taller man took an instinctive step back.

"Then send me back."

"What?"

"You heard me. Send me back—right now!"

"You're joking, Victor," Roschestvensky stammered, then squared his shoulders. "You're bluffing."

"No, I'm not bluffing, Simon. I'll play your little game. I won't go after Gelman. I won't start my own show. But I won't stay away from Tina."

Simon shook his head. "You're crazy, Victor. You'd blow your only chance on that cheap whore?"

Kolnikov's hand shot out and grabbed the other man by the tie, at the same time slamming him back against the door jamb. Then, with the same one hand, he lifted him clear off the floor. Kolnikov's face was that of a gargoyle, Roschestvensky's of a choked blowfish.

"Whether I stay out or go back, Simon, don't ever . . . ever . . . speak to me about Tina. And as long as I'm out, I'm going to see her . . and what's more, I'm going to find your tap and jam it up the ass of the first spook I find tailing me. Understood?"

Roschestvensky nodded readily. He had little choice if he wanted to retain consciousness. Although he was probably responsible for more "terminations" than Kolnikov, he had never made the hit himself; Kolnikov had. Too, Simon had the underlying fear-respect which the aristocrat feels for the peasant; one-on-one, the borzoi is no match for the bear.

Kolnikov set him down.

"I'm sorry, Simon, but I meant what I said. Either that, or I go back."

Twenty minutes later, Captain Roschestvensky departed the hotel. Five minutes later, Victor Kolnikov emerged, shaved and dressed and with his kit bag in his hand. He hailed a cab and gave the driver the East Side address of Tina Vivaldi's apartment.

EIGHT

CAPRICIOUS SPRING had decided to tantalize New York City with a foretaste of pleasures yet to come. As if with the wave of a wand, she had swept away the gray rains. The sun, its face freshly washed, shone down from the middle of a perfectly cloudless blue sky. It was hard to believe that yesterday had ever been. Every New Yorker who could have deserted his or her steel and glass and concrete winter prison to savor the sudden warmth, and the lively chatter and lightened footfalls mingled with the calls of delighted birds. Only the leaves and flowers chose to remain aloof; like wary groundhogs, they would give nature a few more weeks to prove her good intent.

Victor lounged on the left end of a park bench just north of the sparkling glassiness of the United Nations Plaza well in sight of the East River. He studied its bustling commerce, pausing occasionally to nibble on a foot-long hot dog or to raise his pale face to the hot, piercing rays from above. An open newspaper lay draped across his knee. Like one too quickly roused from sleep, he was giving his soul time to catch up with the events of the past two days. He was meeting with only halting, almost timid, success. Almost too much had changed, and too quickly.

Even the hot dog. Not good, wholesome Navy chow served on a steel tray according to the Navy's immutable timetable, but obtained when he chose to have it. Not boiled and served up with the inevitable beans, but grilled to a crisp. On a bun, wrapped in wax paper with his *choice* of condiments—the works, including sauerkraut. He finished it, signaled for another from the owner of the nearby stand, and took up his paper.

In Portsmouth, their jailers had denied them even the news, as if just knowing what was going on in the world outside would contaminate it. Their only tidbits had come to them with Simon's infrequent visits or via the stray comments of the guards. Now, three Presidents later, there was a lot to find out; it made him feel like Dreyfus, which set his mind again toward Gelman. He shook his head, almost physically trying to set the thought aside. Gelman was no longer his prey. Time enough for that, later. Better, perhaps, to plan some time in the public library leafing through back issues of *Time*.

An item about Admiral Rickover struck his eye. So the old man was finally retiring. Forced into retirement, actually. And in passing, he had leveled one of his famous broadsides at stupidity, inefficiency, and ineptitude in the Defense Establishment. Curiously, Rickover had also condemned nuclear power in general—both military and civilian —as too dangerous for mankind in any form. Victor found this amusing. He had met the Navy's reigning genius on three occasions and had acquired a grudging admiration for the diminutive firebrand's dedication, if not his tact. He recalled a story he had heard that, when the future father of the nuclear Navy had graduated from Annapolis, his photograph and write-up had been placed all by itself in the middle of a page, printed on one side only. And that single page had been perforated along the gutter, so those who wished to *could remove it without damaging the rest of the yearbook!* Times hadn't changed all that much since 1923. Jews were barely tolerated in the wardroom. Most were looked upon as being leftists, if not Communists, especially since the Rosenberg case. How Gelman had gotten as far as he did was a mystery. Though not really; he was a genius *with* tact.

Actually, until he began to uncover Gelman's possible role as long-term plant in the system, Victor had not particularly hated him. Not like Gruber or some of the others had. He remembered his own father's stories about the treatment of Jews under the Czars. They had been conscripted, often to be separated for life from their homes and families, and forcibly converted to Christianity. That they might already have wives or children did not matter; the Czar's minions seemed to search out these "especially eligible" young men. Therefore, hatred of all things military could be understood if not wholly forgiven in the context of their new homeland. At least for Easterners. But why Gelman, a German? German Jews had been almost totally "assimilated," as the term goes, many serving as officers in the Kaiser's army before the Nazis had changed all that. Maybe that explained it. Christ! Here he was thinking of Gelman again. Victor left the news section for the unthinking amusement of the comics just as a large yellow ball sailed over his paper and onto his lap, followed by a little boy whose hair matched the ball. Victor tossed it back. The child caught it and stood there studying him.

"Are you a Russian?"

"What?"

"Are you a Russian?" The boy's green eyes surveyed Kolnikov appraisingly. "My father says a lot of Russians work in there." He pointed at the nearby buildings.

"No," Victor replied with a smile. "I'm an American."

"You sure look like a Russian. My name's Joshua. My father's a writer and he knows all about those things."

Victor chuckled. "I'm certain he does, Joshua. I'm not Russian, though my mother and father were both Ukrainians."

"Oh. Then you're not a spy." The boy was visibly disappointed.

"No, I'm not a spy."

"Do you work in there?"

"No. Actually . . . I don't work at all. And not because I'm rich, but because I'm temporarily out of work."

The boy, having reached the natural limits of an average child's attention span, thanked Victor for returning the ball and rejoined his waiting playmates.

It was another first in nine years. Talking to a child. Not that Victor had ever given them much thought. Few in his specialty married, except late in life. Not himself. Not Roschestvensky. Not Gruber. Wives and children left a man vulnerable to all sorts of unthinkable possibilities. Only Lowell would have married because he wasn't career, a short-timer doing his tour of duty before returning to the normal life—until caught up with his colleagues in Gelman's net. Damn Gelman!

What was the use? After nine years of hating the man, even the sudden, really unexpected opening of Victor's cherished "alternate plan" wasn't enough to let him stop. Where was Gelman? And his co-conspirators, Horn and Stoddard? What was going down—what could be so big that Simon would risk springing three convicted "traitors," taking such a longshot chance on his own career? And at this particular moment? Victor tried to scan through the relatively small amounts of news he had absorbed the last two days for a clue. Nothing stood out. Basically all the same troubles— a Soviet clampdown in Eastern Europe; Israel and the Arabs; a dispute between Turkey, Bulgaria, and the USSR complicated by the usual bickering with Greece. Afghanistan was new, but quiet. Iran had given back the American hostages and was busy fighting Iraq. All the usual saber-rattling resulting in little more than pinpricks.

Roschestvensky had given no inkling—not during his visits, not now. At Portsmouth, he had quickly rebuffed Victor's probings. That hurt. If he and Gruber and Lowell were to play sitting ducks, at least they should have gotten some handle on how to look out for the hunters. Kolnikov would have preferred the role of fox in the chicken coop, one more befitting his nature. But then maybe the very fact of their release would accomplish that same end: sowing doubt, fright, even panic in Gelman's camp and causing it to run in unplanned directions—one of them right into Simon's trap, whatever that was.

The children's ballgame progressed noisily around and through the evershifting obstacle course of passersby. Twice, the ball came sailing onto the bench; twice, Victor retrieved it, sending it back into play like a pickup referee.

But just what *was* Simon's trap? Simply turning Victor loose on Manhattan, free to roam, didn't seem plausible. Where were Gruber and Lowell sited? Better to have taken all three into Washington, right into the Holy of Holies. No. Not that. It would only chase their targets back to ground. Again, Simon was right—as he had been from the first. One could only draw Gelman's group out, and the further the better. Simon had been right from the beginning. It was his suspicions, expressed to Victor, that had started them all on Gelman's trail nine years earlier. Gelman, the genius counteroperative who had broken one ring after the other in a seemingly endless chain of successes, building for himself an unassailable reputation in the Bureau—until Simon observed a basic similarity: all the successes involved small fry, the expendables an enemy which wished to penetrate deeply would gladly sacrifice. And once they started to dig, the pattern was clear. They had built an almost ironclad case.

Until it disappeared! Every file, every tape, every inch of film, only days before Gelman & Company had played their own hand—*an airtight case against the hunters!* And what a case! Nearly every point they had built against Gelman had been turned against *them*. Even Simon was tainted. Standing by, his friends through the court-martial had hurt him even more. Victor thought of the four stripes. Only four. Simon, perhaps the only man who could have outwitted and outflanked Gelman, would have had his stars by now and been a Deputy Chief of Intelligence had he abandoned his team. And now, unless he wins this one last round, he'll be lucky to retire a captain. As it was, he was lucky to get even that far; he could have been deadended at Commander.

The intensity of Victor's musings had caused him not to notice the man who had taken a seat further down the bench. Now he chanced to glance over at the long, unmistakable profile of Simon Roschestvensky. He does look like a borzoi, thought Victor, those lanky, fast Russian wolfhounds so favored by the Czarist aristocracy until the Revolution had nearly wiped out both. Somehow, it was historically fitting that one of their so brutally diminished breed should still be chasing the human spawn of the Revolutionaries after more than three generations. Simon was concentrating on the river. He didn't even glance at Victor, but spoke as if he simply sensed the latter's attention.

"Lovely day for a walk," he observed quickly over steepled fingers and, lifting himself up with the studied grace of a crane, strolled away toward the nearest crosstown street. Kolnikov caught up with him halfway between First and Second Avenues. Simon was in mufti, wearing a grey chalkstripe suit that accentuated their differences in height and build; its tailormade cut and quality, complete with real buttonholes on the sleeves, made Victor feel shabby by comparison. If he spoke first, Victor felt he might even be taken for a panhandler. Finally, Simon looked down.

"Where's Tina?" he asked as casually as one executive might ask after another's wife.

"She had an errand this morning. We're meeting later. To go shopping . . . for clothes for me." Simon's survey of his shorter companion bespoke agreement with that necessity.

"That would be an improvement. But does it have to be with her?" Victor stopped. Simon took his arm and nudged him back onto their leisurely pace. Simon had something to discuss, else he would not have contacted him so openly. And the UN Plaza was no place to talk, covered as it must be with every listening device imaginable. Even keeping on the move through the cacophony of midtown Manhattan was not a sure bet.

"We agreed . . . or rather, I told you, Simon,

that's not part of the deal. So forget it."
Victor's eyes studied their reflections in the
window of a clothing store. He winced. He
couldn't wait to get out of those rags that
made him look like a parolee with only a
fresh ten-dollar bill to his name.

Simon sighed almost angrily. "Have it your
way, but if it fouls up our plans . . ."

"It won't. What's more, they may not work
—as you said yourself. Then where am I?
Back inside with absolutely nothing to show
for it. And while we're on the subject, why
are you here and how did you find me? A
tail?"

"No. *They're* tailing you . . . or are at the
moment—*DON'T LOOK AROUND!*" he fairly
shouted through his teeth. "You really are
out of practice, aren't you . . . and *we're*
tailing *them*. And to say that they're getting
nervous would be a gross understatement."

"Where's Gelman and the rest . . . incidentally, what's *his* rank nowadays—Rear
Admiral?" Simon's eyes narrowed, making
Victor regret what must be a painful suggestion.

"They're out."

Victor almost broke stride. "*Out?* Where?"

"Gelman went out on twenty—as only a
Commander incidentally—surprised everybody. Moved over to a top job at DIA, then
just quit about a year ago and moved up to
Scarsdale. Says he's going to write a spy
novel and get rich like John Le Carré." Both
men chuckled. "Horn and Stoddard resigned
. . . said they were fed up with the life. Horn's
been selling real estate out of Silver Springs.

Stoddard spent two years as an advisor to a member of the Senate Armed Forces Committee."

"Then why now? Why are we baiting a trap now, if they're out?"

Roschestvensky turned north on Lexington Avenue. Kolnikov wheeled with him, staying close to catch the other's words.

"Because, Victor, they have a follow-on team in place behind them. And the three of them have disappeared." Kolnikov struggled to stay calm. This was like the old days—with Simon, on the hunt, together. It was almost enough to make him consider abandoning the alternate plan, or postponing it until later.

"Disappeared?"

"Completely. Gelman told his neighbors he was going to South America for several months' research. Bought a ticket to Buenos Aires, but never made the flight. That was four months ago. One of our people thinks he took an earlier plane to Lisbon, but we found nothing but a cold trail. Soon after, Horn and Stoddard slipped away. Horn on vacation, Stoddard on an extensive leave of absence."

"And you haven't tracked any of them?"

"Not a one. And rather embarrassing too, I might add." Kolnikov could imagine. It wasn't like his former chief to be caught so flatfooted. One, maybe two, but not all three.

"Which brings Gruber, Lowell, and me into it." Victor smiled. "And if our 'friends' already have the scent . . ." He stifled the impulse to look for their tail, almost expecting to see Gelman in person. But if he had, could he have controlled himself?'' . . . you can sniff back. Where are Gruber and Lowell?''

"Where they'll create the most confusion. Three of you in separate places will triple the drain on their manpower *and* the number of trails leading back. I'm forced to be like an ice fisherman. Three separate lines through the chophole may just bring up one of the big fellows. Now about Tina: do you think you want to expose her?''

And before Kolnikov could frame his thoughts for an answer, Simon waved casually and was off at a fast clip through the milling lunchtime throng.

Victor continued at a slow amble, inspecting first one shop window, then another. It was now less than twenty minutes before he was to meet Tina at the entrance to Brooks Brothers. For a moment, he debated going back to the apartment, collecting his gear, and moving back to Fleabag-on-the-Hudson.

But then, if they were on to him, they must be on to her. In which case, the best thing would be to stay close, where he could protect her. Finally, still with lingering doubts about which emotion had the upper hand, chivalry or desire, he squared his shoulders and headed quickly—one might say eagerly—toward their rendezvous.

NINE

KOLNIKOV TURNED north on Lexington Avenue to Forty-second, then west under the viaduct connecting Park Avenue with Grand Central Terminal. Suddenly he veered into the concourse entrance surprising several other pedestrians with whom he collided. Inside, he slipped into a telephone booth. He pretended to make a call. He watched instead for telltale signs of being followed.

No one hurried to catch up. No cars slowed as they passed. No eyes scanned the marbled interior in search of the sudden fugitive. Nothing. Either nobody was following him—neither Gelman's *nor* Roschestvensky's people—or they were monitoring intersect points only, like Tina's apartment house. Maybe Simon really did trust him. Maybe Gelman hadn't picked up the trail yet. Maybe he was rusty, though all the old routines were flooding back into his consciousness.

He gave it a few more minutes, then slipped out, threading through the hurrying crowds in the great, cavernous basilica like any other eternally urgent New Yorker. And again, before exiting from the Forty-third Street side of the complex, he checked. Unless someone had engaged an infinity of taxicabs and ordered them to keep circling and honking along the street, all seemed clear. New York was the perfect place to spot a tail if you moved slowly, because anyone not in a rush stood out. Still, knowing you are hunted is not unlike Emerson's dictum: "Commit a crime, and the world is made of glass." Half the world here was literally made of glass, and Victor could imagine that every reflecting sheet of it hid an infinity of eyes trained on him. The cheap clothes didn't help.

Victor was deliberately late for his appointment with Tina.

So was she. So much the better. The better to take up position by the window inside a corner coffeeshop where he could command clear fields of view toward all likely approaches to Brooks Brothers' entrance. He knew he would have ample time. Tina was the classic Latin, right down to her idea of "on time." He rested his cup on the standup shelf, his eyes scanning the kaleidoscope of passersby for . . . what? Anything. Even a familiar face, though after nine years the soldiers would have been long promoted from the street, replaced by new "warm bodies" in the ranks.

Simon *could* have been a little more open. Victor found his old natural curiosity gnawing at his psyche. What was going down? What was so big? He wished he knew more, if only in order to avoid a misstep when the time to make his own move arrived. He even found himself regretting the imperative of his own plan. Maybe he should wait? Play Simon's hand out to a grand slam? No. That last thought sounded too much like "slammer," which was where he would find himself again if this scheme didn't work—with his golden opportunity forever lost. And that wouldn't do. Not now. Not after what had been nothing more than an impossible dream concocted to lighten the length of days in prison had been dropped in his lap. He remembered Simon's first words: "How would you like to get out?" Most of the rest had had to filter through a mind suddenly thrown into high gear.

Victor realized that he was sweating. He pulled several paper napkins from the dispenser, wiping first his brow, then his clammy hands. He was hyperventilating. He lit a cigarette and inhaled deeply. He puffed several more times, steaming it down to the obvious annoyance of a middleaged woman who moved ostentatiously away. Victor returned her scowl with a solicitous smile. She was wearing a button in the shape of a European stop sign over a cigarette. Not my type, thought Victor; stingy with the little pleasures, stingy with the big. Stingy body too. Probably live to a hundred, or until all that extra pure air made her faint into the path of a subway train.

Victor continued the battle of expressions until the corner of his eye caught the unmistakable sight of Tina sweeping down Madison Avenue. She wore no coat over the soft flow of her dress, forcing even the jaded natives to do all manner of odd dances in order to achieve a better look. Victor looked too—for those who would be trying too hard not to. Again nothing, unless one counted a catty upsweep of the face here and there.

Kolnikov let Tina stand outside the store for nearly ten minutes while he searched for the telltale signs of covert pursuit. Carefully he surveyed every movement, every nuance of passersby on the busy street. Nothing. No telephone trucks stopped to service a nearby building; no cars interrupted their impatient, honking progress. No one took up station. Either I'm very rusty or they're very good, he thought. Or I shook them. Maybe Simon's mistaken. Forty-eight hours may be too soon for them to have caught up. Or too soon to chance being picked up. But then, Simon said we were being tailed. By his own people perhaps, just to keep me honest? He shuddered. Not seeing was intolerable to a professional; there were only so many possibilities when conducting a tail and he knew them all. Unless surveillance were set up in one of the buildings or someone was waiting inside of Brooks Brothers? Impossible . . . unless Tina was in with Roschestvensky. Victor chuckled. It would be just like Simon, the master spymaster, to know that he, Victor, would probably head straight for her—and then set her up as his keeper. In which case all the hassle and bullshit about their liaison was smokescreen. With him squarely and safely in a wired honey pot, Simon could relax, using his watchdogs where they were needed most.

All the better! he mused. If Simon feels secure, all the easier to split when the time comes. Yes. Victor would certainly go along, veritably wallowing in the honey whilst he and Simon fenced over the "unauthorized" arrangement. Oh, how he would wallow! His searching gaze zeroed back to Tina standing in front of the building, her exquisite feminity gracing the revealing folds of her clothes, the churning welling up from his guts telling him he would much rather be performing than shopping. This was certainly going to be one of the fastest, most decisive shopping sprees on record.

"I'm late and you're even later," Tina proclaimed with feigned annoyance as he kissed her cheek absentmindedly.

"Sorry. I got engrossed in the sights and lost track of time."

"Careful, dearest," she retorted over her shoulder as she entered the door he held for her, "or you'll get yourself taken for a tourist. Next thing you know, somebody'll try to sell you a boat trip on the Circle Line."

"That's not a bad idea. I've never seen New York that way."

"Neither've I. Why don't we do it . . . today, after we're done here."

"Not unless they rent private cabins." He gave her a pat. "We'll go tomorrow morning —*after* breakfast."

"You're incorrigible."

"Not to mention insatiable." They ambled toward a knot of people waiting in front of a bank of elevators, Victor once again trying to bring his senses into tune with the sheer variety of visual stimuli taken for granted by people on the outside. Here and there he spied a price and was shocked. Not that he was a stranger here or in other good stores;

his uniforms had always come from Jacob Reed's Sons in Philadelphia and had always cost twice as much as those sold in the Navy Uniform Shops. In fact, he had spent twice his initial uniform allowance when he had been first commissioned. It had been part of having arrived, the kid from Manayunk buying at the best store downtown.

"Let's hope the weather's as nice as today. It'll be miserable out there this time of year if it isn't."

"Then we'll just have to stay home and amuse ourselves," Victor countered. "Know any good parlor games?" The suggestion riled up his insides again. What was there about this particular woman? She was no more beautiful than scores of others he'd known. Yes, she was wild in bed, but so were a lot of others. What made this one so irresistible—yes, irresistible? He liked most any kind of woman and desired more than just a few. But something . . . something about this one made every nerve in his body stand on tiptoe. Just to see her, to speak to her, to hear her voice over the phone, just to *think* about her made his balls—he recalled the words of a Navy colleague who had (unsuccessfully) yearned for her—"feel like they wanted to crawl right up your asshole!"

"Not in the parlor, darling." Her voice, warm and throaty, cut his reverie short. "Remember the neighbors." The Brooks Brothers elevator was crowded uncomfortably, leaving three latecomers to wait for the next. "You know," Tina continued, idly watching the lighted numbers slowly tick off their progress, "there's a story about a new British ambassador to the United Nations who was given a Circle Line tour of Manhattan, then asked what he thought of the city. And he replied that, from his vantage point on the boat, he had discerned that New Yorkers did only three things: defecate, fornicate, and eat oranges." Victor smiled knowingly. A matronly type shot them a disapproving glare. Victor smiled at her. "Do we have any?"

"Any what?"

"Oranges."

"No."

"Let's pick some up on the way home."

The door opened at the "Men's Suits & Outerwear" floor. "And two dozen raw oysters," Victor added with a parting smirk at the matron.

"By the way," Tina whispered as they edged out the door, "I spotted you in the coffeeshop."

Victor felt the flush on his face. Could it be? After all, it was nine years, plenty of time for Simon to have been running her in his own stable. What *had* she been doing? He thrust his thoughts, and his doubts, aside, covering his reaction as best he could as he followed her through long aisles of suits to an impeccably dressed salesman who greeted them pleasantly. Or almost so, or half so. An openly approving look for Tina, one of less than complete approval for Victor. Suddenly he was back in Jacob Reed's twenty years ago, the poor kid from Mill Street rubbing shoulders with Main Liners and prep-school types from Chestnut Hill—full of Dutch courage propped up by a piece of paper from Congress and rubberstamped by the President proclaiming him an "officer and a gentleman." There was no Tina with him back then. He remembered tying to muster all the command presence he had been taught, almost blurting out (or so it seemed at the time), "A set of Naval officer's uniforms. I want to buy a set of Naval officer's uniforms." Christ! he had thought, cowed by that supercilious bastard who had waited on him then, what if he doesn't believe me! He was already reaching for his wallet, for his ID card, ready to dash out back out through the ornate bronze doors onto Chestnut Street, back to the comfort, the social safety of the Navy Exchange, when he heard . . .

"Yes *sir*." (Unbelievable! He had actually said "sir" to *me* . . . me, Victor Kolnikov from a little row house overlooking the Schuylkill!) "What can I show you?"

"A uniform . . . yes, a set of Naval officer's uniforms."

"A what?" Two voices in unison. Tina and the salesman were staring at him. Victor blushed. All the way to his bottom, just as he had twenty years ago. He regained his composure with difficulty, making a supreme effort to laugh. It was not convincing, at least not to him. "Excuse me . . . er, something in stripes, I think." He shot a glance at Tina, who was regarding him quizzically.

"What size, sir?" Sir! Again that word he

had not heard addressed to him in what seemed a lifetime. Not since they had taken back that paper, the one that made hundreds of thousands of fellow human beings address him thus. How strange it is. A piece of paper, a uniform, some cloth and thread and brass buttons and the world suddenly . . .

"What size do you wear, Victor?" Tina had her hand on his arm. "He needs to know your size."

"I . . . er, I'm not certain. I think a forty-four regular." He regarded the salesman cautiously. I'll bet I can read his thoughts: Mommy's bringing you in for a new suit. Now behave and tell the nice man your size. And don't embarrass me.

Victor wished he were back out on Madison Avenue.

"Right this way, sir."

They followed. The salesman pulled a suit from the rack and led them over to a three-way mirror, helped him off with his Navy-issue suit coat and held the new one for Victor to slip into. He liked the transformation. Four gold stripes and stars on navy blue wouldn've felt even better, would've looked better too. Somehow, though, the face still wasn't what he'd seen matched to suits like this on the streets outside; a briefcase would look even stranger. Damned if he didn't still look like . . . though maybe they'd take him for a Soviet diplomat at the U.N.

"How do you like it?" The question was really directed at Tina.

"I guess . . ." Victor began as the salesman gentled his frame around to view the effect from the back. "I guess it's . . ." For want of anything more intelligent to do, he lifted the left arm and glanced at the price on the sleeve.

"Borzhemoi!"

TEN

VICTOR ROSE LATE and padded out of the bedroom toward the aroma of food cooking. Tina, already dressed, was bent down in front of the oven testing an enormous casserole. She straightened up and smiled.

"Eggs florentine, darling. Mashed potatoes, spinach, and eggs baked with a cheese and cream sauce . . . with an additional Tina touch—sliced sausage." Kolnikov leaned against the door jamb and faked a groan of pain.

"You're going to make me fat."

Tina crossed the short space and kissed him demurely. "Fear not, lover, I'm just barely feeding the fires."

She pressed herself against him. There was no doubt about one fire she *was* feeding!

Victor glanced past her shoulder at the table. It was set for two—complete with candles. For *breakfast?* he mused. He slipped past her and, picking up the candles, placed them on the sideboard.

"What's the matter?"

"I don't like the way the table's set." He scooped up the waiting plates, the silverware, the glasses, the place mats, piling everything haphazardly next to the candles. When all was gone, he turned and crooked a finger at Tina.

"Now c'mere." He reached out and drew

her up in front of himself, her back to the table. "Now, I'm going to show you *my* idea of breakfast." He bent her unresisting body back until she lay across the table before him, like some human sacrifice. "Not here, Victor. Remember the neighbors." She feigned struggle, then resigned herself to being the first course.

Deftly, he slipped off the flimsy panties, revealing a delta of rich auburn, and in almost the same motion lofted her sleek, tanned legs over his shoulders. He crouched down and kissed her brimming wetness, breathing deeply of her warm, musky scent. She struggled.

"No, darling. Let's do that in the bedroom. Remember the neighbors!"

Victor raised his face and regarded her across a rumpled landscape of silk shimmering in the morning sun. "Screw the neighbors!"

Tina stopped struggling and grinned at him. "Me first."

Victor's lips found her labia, his tongue darting firmly, urgently between them. Tina let out an agonized moan. Her hands pressed against his forehead. He wrapped his arms around the tops of her thighs, grasped the entreating hands in his, and redoubled his efforts.

"Oh, my God! Victor, I can't stand it. I . . ." A long shriek echoed off toward the living room. Victor shifted his face, now bathing his nose, his whole face in her. His mouth returned to her *mons venus*, erect and distinct, very distinct now. He sucked it in past his lips, past his teeth, where his tongue could rasp it like a high-speed grinding wheel. Tina kept time with its motion, her long legs kicking wildly, her heels now colliding with Victor's lower back, now pressing in unison against it as her quivering torso arched up off its altar to love in response to a particularly excruciating orgasm. Now she was begging—please! enough! no more! "I can't stand . . . I . . . oh, Victor, darling . . ." Then yet another groan or cry or . . .

Then suddenly Victor was standing, Tina's calves resting on his shoulders. She lay before him like a doll with half its stuffing out. Her eyes were closed, her long, slender neck arched. Aftershocks were still rippling through her supple form when he entered her. Slowly, deliberately he glided into her raging furnace. Her eyes opened briefly, then closed. She was beyond sound.

Now, just as slowly, just as deliberately he began the measured ritual. Another explosion wracked the now-silent Tina. She threw her head from side to side, her lips parted, bereft of the strength to hold them closed.

"Oh God, Victor, I can feel you in my throat!"

Then her hands found the strength to find Victor's hips, urging them on to a faster tempo. "Yes. Yes. Now it's your turn."

Quicker. Much quicker now.

Soon he felt it welling up inside. His lips framed a single word:

"NOW!"

Tina's eyelids flew open, wide with

suddenly unbearable sexual agony. Her hands found his, her nails digging into his palms as his releasing passion spent itself, hotly drowning the last searing flames of desire. Neither closed their eyes. Tina's lips framed three words:

"I love you."

Victor replied in kind.

ELEVEN

VICTOR ABSENTMINDEDLY fingered the flyer the earnest young man on the street had pressed on him as he was walking to his rendezvous with Roschestvensky. At the top, two haggard-eyed children set against a sketch of the standard mushroom-shaped cloud stared hauntingly out at the reader. The headline below them proclaimed: STOP THE NEUTRON BOMB—NOW! Further down, a mass rally in Central Park was announced for the following Sunday.

Fools! Victor thought to himself. Things haven't changed that much in nine years. Maybe only the hemlines and tie widths. Styles, but not substance. The same old but unrelenting campaign—the Great Twentieth Century Children's Crusade, led by Moscow's eager dupes—whole divisions leading vast legions of subordinate Judas goats—marches on. The masters of the Kremlin push the buttons, the vast apparatus of the KGB swings into action, and Bingo! their minions turn out in their millions wherever and for whatever the new Czars direct.

Not that most would believe this was the way it happened. Certainly not that clean-cut, well-dressed young fellow . . . from where? Probably an Ivy League school judging from his appearance; certainly from the cut of his expensive blazer and oh-so-right khaki chinos and costly loafers, shined to military perfection (by a family retainer, no doubt). The same for his girlfriend, who tried so hard to hide her prettiness behind ugly, owlish glasses and an unadorned severity appropriate, so she must have thought, to the deadly seriousness of her Holy Cause.

Clearly New England, both of them. Or Philadelphia. Why was it, he mused, that the Puritans and Quakers seemed to feel it their duty to oppose their country on nearly everything? But such must be the arrogance of moral certitude. Or is it merely an arrogation of leadership of *any* cause with a suitably "moral" tag on it? Now that the officer class is no longer their exclusive preserve, now that the march of true democracy has brought the latecomers into the wardroom and onto the quarterdeck, commissions in the services are no longer fashionable, no longer an unalloyed *cachet* of social superiority. Obviously, the services are then tainted. So, Hell No! We won't go! Better for the mother of a Massachusetts governor to make a fool of herself getting arrested at an antiwar rally; after all, who respects the Social Register—even the social contemptuously call it the *stud book*—anymore? No. The action's in being anti. After all, didn't New England vehemently oppose the Mexican War? Didn't they oppose the Louisiana Purchase and all the rest of America's "imperialist" march to the Pacific—which, just incidentally, diluted their political power? Oh yes, they certainly opposed slavery; but not the Civil War, fought more to protect the domestic markets for their mills than to relieve their long-suffering black brethren.

"Soviet Russia has pledged not to be first to use nuclear weapons," the young man had proclaimed with the missionary zeal of a Jehovah's Witness delivering a verse of holy scripture. "That's right," his mate chimed in, "Andrei Gromyko said it publically at the United Nations." As if that august body were the Council of Nicaea.

Victor had stopped, curious, to read the flyer.

"The neutron bomb is the ultimate weapon of the capitalists," the girl had assured him. "It lets them kill the workers without damaging their property; then they can take it away," she concluded with a nod of absolute certitude.

"The capitalists really want to kill all the workers?" Victor had queried.

"Oh, yes. Then there's nobody to stop them from taking *all* the wealth." She took in the whole world with a sweep of both arms.

"But capital is based on labor. If the capitalists kill all the workers, there'll be nobody to produce their wealth." A nod. "Young lady, are you telling me that Henry Ford II will slaughter all his workers just so he can seize their homes and cars and washing machines and television sets? What does he do *then?* Run around an empty Detroit . . . leave his mansion in Grosse Point so he can move into a different tract house each day—or each morning, afternoon, and evening—driving a different Chevrolet or

Pontiac or Mercury or whatever from house to house—what does he do if there's more than one car, bring his family along to drive them? Or does he move twenty thousand TV sets into a huge auditorium, turn them all on at once—and blow all the fuses?" He had started to guffaw openly at their discomfiture, which was fast growing into hostility, the hatred of the zealot for a clever theologian.

"But you look like, er . . . a, er . . . one of the workers," she stammered angrily, a sense of betrayal glittering in her accusing eyes.

"You mean I look like a foreigner. Not like the Ivy League WASPs *you* grew up with," Victor chortled mockingly, deliberately thickening a stage-Russian accent with each succeeding word. "You are saying I look like dumb Bohunk leevink down beek heel from Datt's beek house on top. No? You sayink this bum in sloppy soot, this Ukey luke like one of glo-r-i-o-u-s pipple you wantink to safe from dirty running-yellow-dog capitalist h-oppressors. You safe him lak leetle black brother in African chunkle—like nice white lady missionary, huh?" He guffawed. "Listen, little lady. My mother and father were from the Ukraine—Ukies, as your kind called them—and my father worked all his life—like a dog —in a mill. To make enough money to raise his family in a two-by-four row hovel in Manayunk—on a hillside so steep the cross streets were stairways. And you want to tell me the mill owners want to move into *our* house?" He roared, holding his sides in mock pain, actual tears flowing down his rough

70

cheeks. He stabbed a thick finger at them. "Tell that shit to your pansy boyfriends from Harvard—not to a *real* worker. *We're* too busy getting rich . . . b͏ ͏ming dirty capital- ists!"

"Fascist pig!" she hissed as they shrank away, bundling themselves to each other as if to ward off contamination.

"Let me know when you see a Rockefeller driving a Chevvie instead of a Rolls-Royce— especially a different one every day. *Then* I'll worry." He started away, waving, his mocking laughter cutting through the waves of naked hatred radiating from the couple. Naked hatred mixed with naked fear. They looked as if, any moment, one of them would whip out a cross and thrust it in his direction. No. A hammer and sickle. Yes, definitely more appropriate.

"Stupid peasant!" the girl hurled after him.

"Yes, you're right, leetle girlnik. And dumb Ukey, too. And come Revolution, we poot fantsy-pantsy boyfriend in labor cemp. Maybe work hard in factory like h-onest man. You we poot een whorehouse to h-entertain heroic soldiers in glorious pipple's army. *Nyet?*"

He was still laughing inwardly to himself when he reached the bar nearly two blocks away. Though he was only partly amused. The same people who pulled the strings on those two street puppets were the ones who had pulled the rug from under him. And Gruber. And Lowell.

But why the neutron bomb? Why a *clean*

bomb? You would think all the liberals in the world would cheer it, a nuclear weapon that produced a tiny fraction of the radiation fallout of conventional—*conventional?*—bombs. One would believe they'd take it to their bosoms, at least be grateful for half a loaf. What's there about the neutron bomb that upsets the master puppeteers of Moscow so much they have pulled out all the stops?

The answer, when it hit him, left Victor holding the door to the bar open like a zombie, stupified. Of course! That it's a clean bomb *is* the issue, but not for the "public" reasons—and most people, especially the committed true believers never probe behind the outward reasons, the slogans, and the fear-inspiring buzzwords. The real reason is 60,000 tanks in the Warsaw Pact arsenal, poised to strike into Western Europe against a tenth of that number—or an eighth. A walk-over of the NATO forces, which wouldn't *dare* use the number of conventional nuclear weapons that would be needed to stop them. The fallout from so much shit thrown into the air would be unacceptable; it would poison the whole planet.

But neutron bombs. We could kill the crews of those 60,000 tanks—and the crews of all the other thousands of rocket launchers, armored personnel carriers, mechanized artillery, *and* their armed hordes of troops—with less fallout than from two or three older bombs! *That's* what they don't want! *That's* what's caused them to order their obedient children onto the streets of New York—unknowing, unsuspecting, ignorant, armed only with slogans they've been fed by their "concerned" professors and peers.

Bastards! Victor thought. Though one must admire both the breathtaking scope and sheer professional thoroughness of such "disinformation."

"I don't know how they did it, Victor. I still don't."

"Don't what?"

"Exactly how they managed to turn the tables on you. An airtight case, a mirror image of your own case against them. Turned, files replaced with their exact opposite, names, times, places, everything you had built—one day, a hundred and eighty degrees around. What's that you're reading?"

Kolnikov passed the paper across the dark oak table. Roschestvensky took it. He fished a pair of steel-rimmed spectacles out of his breast pocket, put them on, and moved the paper under the dim lamp that jutted out from the paneled wall.

"What *is* the current situation with the neutron bomb?"

"You mean . . . will we be permitted to deploy it in Western Europe?" Simon continued to read, answering with half his mind. "It's . . . it's out of R&D and into production . . . that stupid son-of-a-bitch Carter held it back . . . nearly . . . nearly three years. But this new President's put it on line again, though the left, here and in Europe, are having apoplexy and it's still up in the air whether NATO—West Germany especially— will let us deploy it. It's the only thing we could use in numbers sufficient to stop a full-scale Warsaw Pact invasion." He stabbed at the flyer with a long, slender finger. "That's why we've got this, though usually they haven't been going directly for the primary target—characteristically. Instead, they've mounted an attack on nuclear weapons in general, over here as well as over there." He handed the paper back. Kolnikov folded it several times into a compact mass, tearing it into small pieces which he then shoved to the outer edge of the table. A busboy removed them along with the contents of the ashtray a few minutes later.

"What are the odds on deployment?" Roschestvensky had taken out a cigarette. Kolnikov took out one of his and lit a match for both of them.

Simon took a puff and blew the smoke into the gloomy void above them. "On land, I'd say less than fifty-fifty. Moscow's going to fight us every inch of the way on this one. It means the near-total neutralization of their tank and armored superiority there. They might even launch a preemptive invasion to stop it."

Victor's eyebrows shot up. His mentor leaned back, spreading his palms flat on the table. "Absolutely, Victor. What would you do if you had all the trump cards, and the other guy was going to take them away from you? Wouldn't you strike first? Like Gelman did to you . . . or we *presume* he did to you?" Victor made a face. "Seriously, do you really think that, if their campaign to do away with *all* nuclear weapons on West European soil fails—*or* if they can't get a quid pro quo . . .

say, our agreement to hold back on neutron bomb deployment in return for turning down the heat . . . if they can't retreat to their pre-planned fallback position, which is what they wanted in the first place—have no doubt about that: that's the aim of this whole new round—that they'll then resort to what they hope will be a limited war in Europe?"

"You really think so?" Less than a week wasn't much time to catch up on the world but, given his training, the main threads were already into pattern. Simon signaled for another round of drinks; he shrugged.

"So far, they're winning. There's already so much shit on the fan we don't dare ask for more—not when we might be lucky just to hold onto the status quo. Which leaves us with two options." Roschestvensky leaned forward prepared to tick off each point on his fingers. "We can try to deploy them secretly, without NATO's knowledge." He shook his head. "That'd be asking for trouble. What're we going to do . . . smuggle a thousand weapons into Germany under our finger-nails? Forget it. Fifty . . . a hundred, maybe . . . more like a couple dozen, if that." He looked around. The lunchtime hubbub covered his words. Besides, they could have been just any two concerned, informed civilians discussing the weather. Obviously Simon felt secure. If there was a tail, if they were being overheard, there was nothing that any sane man couldn't have said. Simon moved on to the second finger.

"That leaves the Navy. They can't tell us what—or what not—to carry on ships. We could beef up our presence in the North Sea area and the Atlantic—we already have. Mainly from missile cruisers or ship-launched cruise missiles than from aircraft carriers. The North Sea's no place for flight ops." They both gave a shudder of recognition. The whole northern region was hell on ships and planes and men for all but a few weeks of the year. "That leaves carriers in the Med. And that still wouldn't work very well because we're talking about an on-the-spot tactical weapon, not the strategic weapons carriers usually carry. It would mean too few launching points, long, too-predictable approach routes mostly over neutral—even hostile—territory." Simon sighed. "Wouldn't work. We'd need ten carriers on station instead of the one-two we have. And they couldn't do anything else. They couldn't risk getting sucked into the Eastern Med to cover a crisis in, say, Turkey or Saudi Arabia or whatever. And even if we did commit to the program, which would take thirty carriers—as you know—in order to rotate the force stateside, it still wouldn't work. By the time those aircraft that did get through arrived, their people'd be so mixed up with ours—at least the first wave or two—they'd have to try and find the rear echelons, if they could, and dump on them."

"So, you're saying it can't be done."

"Not logically. Not effectively. So, unless we can somehow overcome the current anti-nuke campaign on the home front—both home fronts—we're left with our short arms in our hands with no way to use them."

"Bastards!"

"So what else is new? The French beat them in Indo China, they beat the French in Paris. We kick the shit out of them in Viet Nam, they kick the shit out of us in New York, Washington, and L.A."

"Is that why you brought us out?"

"What?" Simon froze, confused momentarily, his cigarette stalled halfway to his lips.

"Is that why you've brought Gruber and Lowell and me out of cold storage? You think this is it? Maybe something . . . something so big, at just the right moment, that it'd get us kicked out of Europe. Or our nukes—all of them—sent back to Go?" Kolnikov let out a soft whistle, then looked puzzled. "But, Christ, Simon, you're talking about sabotage on a massive scale. Our field was classified information, plain old garden-variety espionage." Victor looked over, searchingly. "Or have we . . . you . . . gotten into bigger things?"

"I can't say. All I can tell you is that my antenna says now's the time . . . now—if ever —is the moment to nudge Gelman from an unexpected quarter. Then, if he should panic, he might just tip his hand."

"In other words, we're nothing but stray red herrings, thrown into the soup at random . . . completely at random . . ."

"Not completely, Victor."

"Well on a pure hunch then." Victor was beginning to feel panicky. "Purely on an expendable basis." He felt his anger rising.

"And if it doesn't work . . . you go back to the Bureau . . . we go back to . . ." He couldn't bring himself to say it.

Simon held up his hand. "Victor. You know me better than that. Trust me."

TWELVE

KOLNIKOV LEFT the bar a little after two. Troubled. He didn't trust Simon. Well, personally, he still trusted him with his life. But not with his freedom.

He remembered Roschestvensky's parting words: "Remember, Victor, I'll hang higher if we fail than you will."

Cold comfort! Ten to twenty more years or worse in that gray tomb? He'd rather hang! But what if Simon's plan *did* work? Suddenly, a hand interrupted his thoughtful passage along the street. Victor wheeled, a shock wave reverberating through his body.

The hand was clutching his right arm, a finger on the other hand pointing into his face. Gray eyes flaming in a still-boyish face scrutinized him intently. "Yes, it is! Victor . . . Victor Kolnikov! God! When did they . . . er, what brings you to New York?" The initial question still dominated the eyes.

"You don't remember me. Do you?"

Victor didn't. Not the name. But the face set off instant alarm bells.

"Mike Coselle. Special Ops COMINTELLANT, Norfolk. We worked on finding out why all the missiles malfunctioned during that big Naval review they set up for Kennedy in Sixty-two. Remember the embarrassment?"

Victor remembered. He also remembered Coselle now too.

"Oh, I'm here just for a few days on business," Kolnikov lied, trying to feign nonchalance. "On a professional trip, a teachers' conference, actually." Victor's mind was at war with itself, conflicting possibilities crowding at each other. What would sound plausible? Shit! Coselle can check up on a conference. Why did you say that? Not prepared for this. Now you've done it for sure: come off like a total amateur.

"Really?" The eyes seemed to reach into him, laying his thoughts bare. "You're *teaching* . . . where?"

"Well . . . not teaching, actually. Trying to get a job teaching. Uh . . . mathematics. I'm going to graduate school for my certification."

"Really? That's interesting. Where?"

"At Temple . . . in Philadelphia." Goddamn! Now he *can* check your story, Kolnikov you dumb *kulak!* "That's right . . . now I recall . . . yes." Victor pumped Coselle's hand vigorously, smiling to cover his inward failure at composure. "What are you doing here?"

"Same thing. Just in and out of business."

He was lying, the outgoing smile notwithstanding. "Are you still with the bureau?"

"No. Not since last year. Retired on twenty. I run a security agency up in Connecticut."

Connecticut. Gelman was in Connecticut! Kolnikov computed dates. It didn't wash; Coselle was three years his junior, which made twenty years impossible. So the hounds *were* on the scent! But why flush him this way? They must be desperate.

80

"You have time for a drink?"

"No, not really. Have to catch a train."

"You were going awfully slow for a man with a train to catch. Are you sure? Just one quick one? Or have you reformed after . . . I mean . . . what time is your train?"

"I'm catching the Congressional at four-thirty." Another nail in your coffin! Did the Congressional still leave at that time? Would he know? Better pray to the Holy Virgin of Kazan that it does.

"You've got plenty of time, Victor. Let's go in here." His hand tugged him toward a door from which several executive types were just issuing, full of that animated chatter that characterizes the breakup of a successful business luncheon, the kind that always includes up to a half-dozen martinis of deadly measure. One of them held the door as he and Coselle entered. Coselle's yellow hair picked up fleeting shafts of light from the ceiling as he led the way into the gloom.

"Why don't we grab a booth. C'mon, you've got time. Or, would you prefer the bar?"

"Suit yourself," Kolnikov replied diffidently. Why not? With just short of two hours to train time, a rush job would compound suspicion. He wished he knew the schedules better. Holy Christ, the name of the train had probably changed and changed again in nine years. What did they call it now? No matter. Coselle knew he had lied. Had to. Now, Kolnikov, you just try to be your goodnatured self and go along. Coselle's here for a reason. Try to find out? No. Play dumb, and try to divine it. Victor took a deep breath as he settled in to the comfortable leather bench opposite his newfound inquisitor.

"It must be nine years, now, since . . . er, since your, er . . ."

"Since the trial?" Victor chimed in, completing the question, angling for the initiative, grateful for the younger man's delicacy. "I got out last November. All very quietly. Presidential pardon." Eyebrows arched, the head inclined.

"Were you cleared? I always thought you would be someday. Never believed a word. Not for a minute. What're you having?"

"I think I'll try a martini."

"Gin or vodka?" a voice from above inquired. It belonged to a shapely waitress. Victor regarded her from head to toe. She looked very good. After nine years of not seeing even a picture of one, every woman looked good.

"Gin. With a twist. And make it a double, straight up." Straight up yours would be more like it, he mused.

"I'll have a beer—draft if you have it." The girl turned and left. Going light, Victor observed. All right, I'll play the game; I'll spot you a double to every beer and put you right under the table.

"Well now, that's good news . . . about the pardon, I mean. Were you exonerated?" Coselle had the easy *bonhomie* of a life-insurance salesman. Victor had always been neutral in his personal feelings toward him. Until now. So he was one of them. Or was he? He could simply be under orders. Very likely.

Use a pawn; hold the vital pieces safely in the back rank. On the other hand, he would be too senior—much too senior by now to be a street man. Victor's dislike deepened.

"Would you prefer not to talk about it?"

"About what?" Caught out *again!*

"Your pardon. Excuse me for prying. I don't mean to. It's just that I didn't expect . . ."

"Didn't expect to ever see me again?" Victor smiled. Coselle reddened.

The girl saved the moment. She put the drinks on the table. Coselle lifted his toward Victor. "Well, here's to better days."

Kolnikov raised his glass and continued. "No, I wasn't exonerated—not yet. But there were some anomalies in the case, and my lawyer managed to have the whole thing quietly reviewed. Probable doubt and all that." There! Report back on that!

"What about . . . the, er, other two . . ."

"Gruber and Lowell? They just dropped quietly out of sight." Kolnikov started feeding lines further through Simon's hole in the ice. "I would imagine Lowell's gone back to Boston. Gruber? I can't say where he might've gone. I doubt it was back to Milwaukee. He was the bitterest of all at our treatment," Victor offered. "I wouldn't be surprised if he's in Washington trying to ferret out the truth—or get even," he added with a knowing smile. That's right! Make 'im sweat a little.

If Coselle was sweating over this last bit of information, he didn't show it. He dismissed it with an offhand shrug. "Well, I really couldn't blame him. I always thought something was fishy. Of all the people . . . you three." He shook his head violently. "I just couldn't believe you—or they—could . . . er, could do all the things you were charged with."

"Seven senior officers believed it. The case —on the surface, at least—was foolproof."

"But you didn't . . . rather, you three were innocent . . . well, weren't you?" Coselle's demeanor puzzled Kolnikov. Coselle was either a superb actor, or this was really a chance encounter. But right after walking away from luncheon with Roschestvensky? He found himself wishing Simon was with him right now. Or that he were more open about whom to expect—or what. But then, Simon had to play it close. It was obvious that he had a strong lingering doubt, and cutting Victor in too much on the expected actions or *personae* of the prospective opposition would be stacking the deck. Victor's respect for his old boss was growing, even if Simon's expressed ambivalence was exasperating to an innocent man, even if he were throwing Lowell, Gruber, and himself out like staked game to draw the big cats. And where were Gruber and Lowell? Where were they spotted (I'll know quickly enough when I make my move!) Why me in New York City? Why here instead of Washington? Or is Simon really going off the deep end, running his own private show? In which case, Washington would be too fraught with peril . . . mines everywhere. . . too easy for Victor to be recognized, picked up, have the whole operation blow sky high before it barely got underway. New York was better: far enough away to avoid too many chance encounters, close enough to the action—or rather, close enough to get picked up—like now. Victor suddenly realized that he was staring at a color snapshot. A woman and two children were smiling at him from their vantage point on a suburban-looking lawn.

"That's why I got out, Victor. Intelligence —at least the interesting stuff—is a single man's game. Right?" He looked to Kolnikov for affirmation.

"I guess so. But I've never been married." Coselle nodded his understanding, then lapsed into half-embarrassed, half-don't-know-what-to-say silence. Suddenly he brightened.

"Incidentally! That girl you used to know. Tina Vivaldi?" Victor nodded uncommittally. "She still lives in New York. Met her on the street this past winter. Still a knockout. Maybe you should look her up . . . or have you?"

Simon's warnings flashed through Victor's head; his whole body tensed. He fought to stay relaxed, outwardly calm. "Oh, really? No, I haven't tried. What's she doing nowadays?" A thought flashed. "How do you know Tina, Mike?"

Coselle grinned. Disarmingly? "C'mon, Victor. Lots of us know about her. How could you keep something like *that* classified, much less Top Secret?"

"But you didn't work this area—not then. How could you've come to know her or even about her?"

"Top Secret—classified information, old man. Sorry," Coselle half chortled.

Son-of-a-bitch! Wait . . . hold on, Victor. He's decoying you. *Stay cool!*

"I guess I should look her up," Victor mused. "Did she say where she's staying?"

"Somewhere in New York." Coselle replied with an offhand wave.

"I think I might—next trip." Victor glanced around. "Which reminds me, I better be heading for Penn Station." Coselle checked his watch.

"Oh, you have plenty of time. It's only three-fifteen."

"Yes, but I want to walk," countered Kolnikov. "After all that time, I want to drink in the sights." Coselle let out a slight sigh of resignation.

"I guess you do. Don't blame you." He signaled for the check.

"By the way, Mike, do you have a business card? So I can phone you next time I'm up this way. Maybe we can get together." Coselle fished out a small leather case, instantly slipped out a card, and handed it over.

"Maybe you can come up for dinner. My wife's heard about you. She'd like to meet you."

Sure! Victor thought. She looks about as much interested in convicted spies as I am in bridge parties in . . . he regarded the address on the card . . . Bridgeport. Looked kosher enough. Coselle Security Systems, Business-Industrial-Personal. If it was a prop, they'd thought of everything. He could just hear

Gelman: *"Here're your business cards. If I know Kolnikov, he'll ask for one to see whether you've got it and how you'll react if you don't."*

Coselle paid the check and they parted company out on the street—Coselle eastward, Kolnikov toward the West Side. Now what to do? Tell Simon, obviously. But how? Better to walk to the station. At Fifth Avenue, he turned south. Halfway along the third block, a yellow-and-black taxi drew abreast, its driver leaning out the window.

"Taxi, sir?"

Kolnikov waved him on, and continued walking.

"Taxi . . . sir?"

Victor stopped, then got in without looking back from where he had just come.

"Where to, sir?" the cabbie demanded without even a peek in the rearview mirror.

"Penn Station . . . I guess."

Without a word, the driver ground the transmission into gear, heading down the avenue to the accompaniment of the obligatory New York screech of rubber. Pulling up to the Seventh Avenue entrance in a further screech of rubber, the driver turned to Victor: "That'll be three twenty-five, sir." Victor handed him a five dollar bill.

"Keep the change."

"Thank you, sir. I'll pick you up on the Eighth Avenue side as quickly as you can get there."

"Isn't that risky?"

"He's in a hurry."

Kolnikov exited with misgivings. He

hurried into the entrance, tripping rapidly down the escalator past a score of less eager riders and making a beeline for the Eighth Avenue side. Short of the exit, he sidestepped into an empty storefront searching the long concourse for pursuers. No sign betrayed one. Then, still slightly breathless from his near-run, he stepped out just in time to be re-intercepted by his newfound guardian.

THIRTEEN

ROSCHESTVENSKY WAS waiting for them on the southwest corner of Eighth Avenue and Forty-second Street. He climbed in quickly and ordered the driver to continue north.

"What did he want?" Simon demanded, urgent concern edging his usually calm voice.

"Just wanted to know when I got out, what I'm doing."

"What'd you tell him?"

Kolnikov could feel himself blushing. "I told him . . . I told him I was trying to get a job teaching." And after an embarrassed instant, "And that I'm studying for certification . . . at Temple . . . in Philadelphia."

"Why did you say *that?*"

Victor's blush deepened. "I . . . I don't know. It was the first thing that came into my head."

Simon scowled at him.

"Well, what do you want? He caught me by surprise. After all, I'm not too sharp on this sort of stuff anymore." Victor made a face of angry self-justification and slumped down in the seat. Roschestvensky gazed out at the passing traffic.

"I guess not," he stated half to himself. "What did he say about himself?"

"That he's retired. Running a security out-fit up in Connecticut." Kolnikov fished out the business card and passed it over to his companion. Simon looked at it and grunted. Passed it back.

"Purely a cover story. He's still in. He's a quote-enquote *civilian consultant* to the US Mission to the UN. Primarily, he keeps tabs on spooks—mainly Naval types—in other, unfriendly missions." Roschestvensky kept his gaze directed in front of them. "Did he say anything else?"

Kolnikov hesitated. Simon turned, his eyes intently questioning.

"He mentioned Tina. Said he ran into her this past year."

"And what did you say?"

"Nothing," Victor blurted. "Nothing at all. Said I might look her up sometime."

Roschestvensky shook his head disgustedly. "And *that's* precisely why I told you to stay away from her. She's bad news, Victor. Right now, at least. At the very minimum, she's a hazard; one way or the other, they might be able to get at you through her."

Kolnikov declined to speak. They had been passing Central Park; the Dakota was slipping by on their left when Simon spoke again.

"Well," he exclaimed with a long sigh, "the chase is on."

Victor sat up and fumbled for a cigarette, selected one, and lighted it. Simon silently declined the offer of one, proffered as an afterthought.

"Do you think he's one of them? I mean, could it've been a chance meeting?"

Simon shook his head, his lips smiling,

though not his eyes. "I would guess not . . . a chance meeting, that is. Much too coincidental." Again, a shake. "No. It makes sense. Shooting someone up from Washington would be too obvious." He steepled his fingers under his chin. "Whether he's part of the inner circle . . . I simply don't know . . . for now. But it *is* interesting . . . interesting that they used him instead of someone from District Headquarters. You have been reporting?"

"You should know."

Simon shot him a half-glare. "Anything unusual . . . that is, during your visits?"

"Nothing. The Duty Officer gives me the log and I sign it, just as you told me."

When they reached the top of the Park, Roschestvensky directed the driver to head crosstown to Park Avenue and subsided against the back of the seat, silent, his eyes closed, his arms folded.

At his own request, Victor was deposited at Park Avenue and Sixtieth. Simon had not added any more admonitions to his ongoing concern about Tina and her possible role in their affairs. He hadn't needed to. All that evening, Kolnikov would be assailed by doubts and fears in almost equal number. Was Tina part of it? But then Victor, by his own actions, had made her part of it. And in that case, would she be safe? Would she be safe even if on Gelman's side? If so, what then? What would be his feelings?

Try as he might, Kolnikov couldn't dampen the rush of his thoughts. He would sleep very little that night, even after their vigorous mutual joy in each other, repeated almost hourly in some way or another until she—if not he—lay in a deep, exhausted slumber, limbs akimbo across her bed. Then the very artificial silence of her bedroom would amplify the sounds within Victor's head. Eventually, he would seek the silence brought on by the contents of Tina's well-stocked liquor cabinet.

Morning found him slumped in a corner of the couch, a fresh fifth of scotch less than a third as fresh as when he had attacked it.

FOURTEEN

ON FRIDAY morning, Kolnikov reported to the Duty Officer at Third Naval District Headquarters in lower Manhattan promptly at 0800, as ordered by Roschestvensky the previous Sunday. And as he had done every day that week, he left a few minutes later, having signed the log offered by the Duty Officer without comment.

This morning, however, instead of heading back uptown, he proceeded southward toward the granite bastions of the Financial District. There had been no apparent tail on him on the subway ride down, and none now. Perhaps, he thought, Simon had been convinced by his repeated promises to stay clear of Gelman and not to start his own show. There were certainly bigger fish to fry. But what of the others? Would they chance losing him? Or had they, knowing his morning routine by now, been merely spot-shadowing him, picking him up at one pre-selected interception point after the other. If so, they would be on the scurry from his newest move.

Except for the bickering with Simon over Tina and the encounter with Coselle, this first week out had been almost disappointingly uneventful—unless one counted his "events" with Tina herself. He had spent every tumultuously lustful night with her, and most of every lustfully tumultuous day: moviegoing, shopping, drinking in all the sights and sounds, the smells and feelings of freedom.

Victor now sported a new suit, buttondown oxford cloth shirt, regimental silk tie, and glistening plain black shoes from Brooks Brothers—a gift from his loving Tina and a signal improvement over the Navy issue; she had bundled the latter down the trash chute at her apartment house. A dashing Burberry trench coat, also courtesy of Tina, protected his blue-chalk-striped stylishness from the end-of-March damp which still hung pervasively about him as he strolled leisurely through one narrow-walled canyon after another. The buildings' grayness reminded him of prisons, in this case designed to keep people out rather than in. Still, it made him shudder at recent memories, which even Brooks Brothers were powerless to diminish.

From time to time, he stopped to window-shop the stores which intruded their occasional flashes of warmth and human scale from solitary niches in the otherwise somber solidity of this capital of Western wealth. Too, he couldn't resist admiring his new image reflected in those windows; topped as it were by a natty tweed all-weather hat, his eyes obscured behind large, military-style sunglasses, he looked every inch the fashionably successful spy. The sight also served to reassure him that this was not all a dream, that he wouldn't reawaken on his hard cot, clad in styleless denim, his world a barred cube within other gray walls. The selfsame windows also let him search for a tail.

Finally satisfied that the scurrying throngs of workers swirling past and around his unhurried self contained none but honest men —toward himself, at least—he strode out smartly, finally issuing out into the green-swarded brightness of Battery Park.

The 8:30 A.M. Circle Line excursion boat for Liberty Island was collecting its last few tourists—at this time of day and year, it was only half full—when Kolnikov purchased a ticket and walked briskly aboard to the accompaniment of a tour guide's cheery huckstering about the glories of the Statue of Liberty and Ellis Island.

He was the last to board. No one followed. Why should they? There was only one way back, and when he took it, he could be picked up safely again at the boat landing. Not this time, however.

The idea had occurred to him the day he and Tina had gone "yachting," first around the whole of Manhattan Island, then out the same destination as this morning. A word to her—without explanation—had resulted in a contact with one of her family on the Jersey side, which had in turn set up this morning's "excursion."

Debarking from the wide, white-painted wooden slip, Kolnikov separated from those who followed the hawking guide to the statue's entrance and hiked quickly around to the far side of the island. A solitary man sat hunched over a fishing line suspended over the side of an open dory anchored squarely in the middle of the narrow channel that divided the island from the New Jersey shore beyond. Victor signaled, and the man quickly drew in his line and anchor; then, with a tug, he brought the boat's outboard motor to life, its low juddering echoing dully off the base of the giant statue behind Kolnikov. The man steered to within a few feet of the shore, rising to steady Victor as he leaped in, then headed in a sweeping curve for the opposite side. No words passed between them, and none passed between Kolnokov and the driver of the Jersey City taxi that was waiting for him close by the park which now occupied the former site of a once busy railroad terminal.

Alighting in the center of Jersey City, Kolnikov took a deliberately circuitous route to the transit station on what was commonly known to locals as the PATH lines. From there, it was only a swift few minutes across the Meadows to Newark and an Amtrak train to Philadelphia.

He had trusted Tina. Actually, he had tested her. Why? he thought. God knows. No. It was deeper than that. He *had* to know where she stood. Yes, he had gone to her as much from pentup lust as anything else. But now another long-suppressed and much deeper reason was asserting itself. And he had to know the truth. If she was playing him false, he would spot it on this occasion, and he would still not discuss the true nature of his mission. No one had followed him onto the train at Newark—of that he was certain. But then they would assume him to be heading for Washington, and plan to pick up his trail there. Still, somewhere along the line, there would've been a telltale sign, some small slipup. So far, there was none. And he was pleased.

It was just ten-fifty when he arrived.

When North Philadelphia was still middle-class, prosperous, and orderly, its Roman Renaissance station on North Broad Street was the preferred crossroads of the rich and powerful, of the important and well-known of the city. In the Thirties, the Forties, and even in the Fifties, a continuous parade of classic Cadillacs, Packards, Lincolns, and lesser makes, all chauffered by respectful drivers in neat, black uniforms with shiny-billed caps, met nearly every train.

Now the station was as ill-used as the ghetto surrounding it, as socially fashionable as the winos sprawled on its few unvandal-ized benches. Characteristically, the freshest paint was the graffiti scrawled over every reachable inch of wall, inside and out.

Kolnikov hurried himself apprehensively along the dingy, dripping underground passageway to the adjacent station of the Broad Street Subway, itself a material and human monument to what had become of this once-proud part of Philadelphia.

When he stepped off the bottom of the stairs at the north end of the station, it appeared deserted, save for a youth at the far end who was inflicting his culture on the reverberating void with a radio the size of a briefcase.

Kolnikov moved further up the platform.

97

As he did, a hulking form of menacing mien and proportions stepped out from behind a large blue-tiled pillar and truculently demanded a light for his cigarette.

Kolnikov's mind raced as he reached into his left coat pocket for his lighter. Christ Jesus! Not now! Not here! Damn! He quickly weighed the odds. Getting mugged, perhaps hospitalized, here would completely upset his timetable, maybe even his whole plan. But so would getting busted by the Philly police, though their questions would be nothing compared to Roschestvensky's. Better to be mugged.

Maintaining an outward nonchalance, Victor flicked the lighter in his left hand and passed it close to the other man's face. From under the protective shield of his dark glasses, his eyes searched the other's unblinkingly for any sign of breaking trouble: specifically, that tiny flicker which telegraphs the punch.

It came between the third and fourth puff as the smoke had begun to swirl about their heads. Victor shot his glance down just in time to see it coming up at his chin. He ducked to the right and down as the angry fist rocketed past his left ear; its unstopped force carried the assailant's arm high in the air and arched him backward. His startled eyes, staring at the light bulb above him, couldn't see the hand chopping up between his knees. Not until the pain from his groin announced its arrival with an explosion in his brain that turned the bare, white bulb into a spreading starshell of red and orange and yellow.

He crumpled to the platform with one long, urgent sucking of air, and rolled halfway over, his back exposed to Kolnikov. Taking careful aim now, Kolnikov drove the toe of his spitshined black shoe viciously into the area of right kidney. The big fellow hiccupped loudly—once—then lay motionless; he was mercifully out of his pain, for the moment. He had selected his intended victim unwisely.

Kolnikov glanced around. A middle-aged couple were standing on the bottom step of the stairs from which he had just descended. They were frozen in horrified fascination at what they had just witnessed. Then they moved on down the platform, giving Victor a look of "good for him" as they passed.

The cacophony at the other end of the station had kept the radio owner oblivious to the incident; and the others who arrived ahead of the next train gave the sprawling form the same attention they habitually give to any other derelict.

Kolnikov detrained without further incident at the Race-Vine Station just north of City Hall, and proceeded briskly to his first stop: Adler's Naval Tailors. Sited strategically across from the Armed Forces YM/YWCA on Fifteenth Street, Adler's had been catering to the uniform needs of servicemen in transit for as far back as almost anyone could remember.

A slightly bent-over man of about sixty with steel-rimmed spectacles, rolled shirtsleeves, and bald head surmounting the mandatory symbol of his office, a draped tape measure, waited on him immediately. Kolnikov came right to the point. He had just gotten urgent orders and needed a uniform—right away. He picked out a suit of lightweight officer's blues, a cap with white cover, an inexpensive chrome- and gold-plated officer's cap insignia and gold chin strap, and an array of ribbons consistent with his age and rank. The salesman-tailor chalked up some minor alterations to the sleeve length and waist, and marked the cuffs on the uniform—which otherwise fitted Kolnikov perfectly. The sleeves were to have two and a half gold stripes—Lieutenant Commander—surmounted by a Supply Corps oakleaf device. Everything was in stock; he was promised the completed job in an hour. Time enough.

As he left the store, Kolnikov silently congratulated himself on still being able to come off as an authentic officer after all these years. But then it had been so burned into him that it would never be really lost. He had not even been asked to show the forged ID card or phony set of official orders he had with him.

Kolnikov's next stop was the cavernous art-deco second floor main office of the Philadelphia Saving Fund Society at Twelfth and Market Streets, just five minutes' walk from Adler's.

The willowy young blonde at the art-deco

100

desk with a sign that proclaimed her an Assistant Vice President was politely surprised that it had been so long since Kolnikov had last used his account. But she accepted his current Navy identification and ten-year-old Virginia driver's license as proof of his story about long years abroad busy on the high seas. And she concluded that he was Victor Joseph Kolnikov and entitled to the money in his account. It totalled nearly five thousand dollars, including some two-odd thousand from his share of his deceased parents' estate. Victor asked for five hundred in cash and four thousand in traveler's checks. He got both, and was out in less than forty-five minutes.

Then, after killing a few minutes with a hot dog and orange drink, standing up at a corner eatery, he headed back to Adler's, collected his purchases, bought a cheap, black suitcase to put them in, and left. He hailed a passing cab on J.F.K. Boulevard.

Before heading for the airport, Kolnikov guided the taxi driver to a small, neatly cropped Ukrainian cemetery perched on the steep slopes of Manayunk overlooking the Schuykill just beyond the upper end of East River Drive. He told the cabbie to wait, then labored up the slope, through the open iron gate crowned with an Orthodox cross, to the place where his sister had written him that his mother and father lay buried. He found the simple headstone and placed the small bouquet of flowers he had bought from a street vendor downtown between the graves. Then he knelt and, for the first time in over a decade, crossed himself—from right to left in the Orthodox fashion.

Coming here at just this time meant taking a chance, but this would be Victor's last chance to be near the mother and father he had loved so much. Now, as he knelt, he thought only of them.

Kolnikov's father, Pavel Michailovich, had been fortunate most of his life. One of the trusting young soldiers of the Czar, he was captured early and unhurt by the Germans after General Samsonov's debacle in 1914. He weathered internment with the stolid fatalism of the eternal *kulak*. The Treaty of Brest-Litovsk, however, brought peace to neither Russia nor him. Instead, he was herded straight from the repatriation train into a Motherland wracked anew by the White-Red imbroglio. Issued a delapidated rifle, some ammunition of questionable reliability, and adequate food only occasionally, he was tramped about on the monotonous plains of the Ukraine from one confused melee to the next. Finally, like millions of his reluctant comrades, he simply left his rifle and found his way back to his home village of Bolechov in the northern Carpathians beside an insignificant tributary of the Dniester. Provincial Lvov, 150 kilometers to the north, was a metropolis by comparison.

The daughter he had never seen was nearly six years old when he finally found her cowering from him behind the rude, homespun skirts of her mother, Anna Ivanovna.

But even final peace didn't bring peace. The last treaty found Bolechov across one of those rubbery Balkan borders which have ever been the curse of that region—and in the brave new Polish "Republic," as it was called by optimistic statesmen. But when the well-meaning but politically incompetent republic of Paderewski degenerated into the xenophobic fascist dictatorship of Marshal Pilsudski, the choices narrowed to three: Red Terror, near-certain starvation, or liquidation in a Ukraine being ravaged by the new Soviet aristocracy of Leningrad and Moscow; hatred and religious discrimination in overwhelming Roman Catholic, anti-Orthodox, anti-everybody-else Poland; or emigration to the last shining hope of America.

At least Manayunk was not too foreign. The tongues were the same, and the steep Schuylkill Valley was not unlike those around Bolechov. Pavel Michailovich had acquired only two skills: leading his father's dray horse from door to door as the old man delivered their small farm's surplus foodstuffs to the inhabitants of Bolechov; and fighting—or more accurately, staying alive under the bungling orders of one besotted Czarist or White officer after another. But little skill was needed for the backbreaking labor of pushcarting goods about the ancient knitting mill down by the river.

Three more children and a long interregnum preceded Victor. He was late and loved excessively by his mother, who swore that her precious Vikki would make the family's dreams of success in America come true. And she backed her oath with years of slavery for

103

every penny that went into the little local bank "for college."

And it had once come true—for awhile. A scholarship and degree at the University, a commission in the Navy—an officer *and* a gentleman!—and yet another degree, and another. The learned doctor, officer, and gentleman was Anna Ivanovna's greatest treasure.

That's why it was so hard when it all came crashing down on them all nine years ago.

Kolnikov's father went first and mercifully; he died of a heart attack two days after hearing the verdict of the court-martial. Anna Ivanovna lingered. She had visited him as often as she could, using interest from savings, her husband's small pension, or money begged from embarrassed and reluctant children. And in her heart she never lost faith in her Vikki. But age and shame finally did it. Whether it was harder to bear the open triumph of envious neighbors or the kind, though still condescending, solicitude of friends, she eventually withered into her black shawls of redoubled widowhood and, one night two years ago, wrapped the draperies of broken dreams about her and dreamed no more.

Victor swore as he thought of this. And how Gelman and his circle had sent them to their broken, disappointed end. Arnold Gelman would be someday sped—painfully and slowly, if Victor had his way—to his appointed place beneath the earth he now trod upon so freely and, so far, successfully.

Kolnikov brooded all the way to the airport, then all the way down on the plane to Norfolk.

FIFTEEN

THE TAXI driver in Norfolk recommended a motel only two blocks from the main gate of the Norfolk Naval Air Station; it was clean and adequate, and ideally located. Kolnikov showered, shaved, and changed into his new uniform. With every piece he put on, he felt a little better, stood a little more erect, assumed more the air of an officer and gentleman. When done, he couldn't resist admiring the effect in the full-length mirror. Perfect! It reminded him of the thrill he had felt the first time nearly twenty years ago at Officer Candidate School, Newport; it had almost ranked with his first woman.

He adjusted the rake of the cap, dusted off the shoes—which looked as if they must have been shined by John Paul Jones's personal steward—and was saluted through the gate by the Marine sentry at exactly seventeen-ten. Just in time for Happy Hour.

The bar at the Commissioned Officers' Mess (Open) was filled with the usual Friday night crush of young and not-so-young-as-they'd-like-to-appear officers divided into the usual mix of dress blues and dress mufti. Kolnikov edged through the crowd to the middle of the long oak bar between two convivial groups of junior officers, all sporting the gold wings of the Naval Aviator

—or, as they're commonly called in the Navy, "Airdales."

Tonight Kolnikov was doing the birddogging. And it took him only a few minutes of conversation and a round of drinks to find out what he wanted to know: which supercarrier was presently with the Sixth Fleet in the Mediterranean. He was in luck; it happened to be his old ship, the U.S.S. *Forrestal.*

Having gotten what he came for quickly, and anxious not to stretch his luck, Kolnikov bought one more round, made his apologies to the serious drinkers, and left—out by the same main gate to the salute of the same Marine sentry.

The whole exercise made Kolnikov want to laugh at the farce of so-called "security." Although he carried a valid-looking ID card in the name of Lieutenant Commander Vasyli M. Kolchov, Supply Corps, USN, it had not been requested by the sentry. It almost never was in peacetime. The uniform and a reasonable demeanor were sufficient to let him enter the airbase, plant time bombs on every plane there, and leave unchallenged.

Victor hoped he'd be as convincing when he went aboard the *Forrestal* in Naples—and as fortunate.

He stopped halfway to the motel and bought a Polaroid camera and a pack of film. Further down the block, he spied a store under a huge sign which proclaimed "Package Goods," the Commonwealth of Virginia's quaint hypocrisy for booze. He bought a fifth of Stolichnaya.

He would have preferred the warmth of Tina. But tonight, he would content himself with the Kulak's Comrade.

SIXTEEN

THE DUTY Yeoman at Headquarters, Commander, Naval Air Forces, Atlantic, was sleepy but respectful to the officer who presented himself at 0810 Saturday morning and requested the name and home address of the *Forrestal*'s Disbursing Officer—and very helpful. Such information is supposed to be confidential, but third-class petty officers who hope to make second-class anytime soon are wise not to pose too many minor objections in the way of senior officers, no matter how irregular the request. In less than ten minutes, Kolnikov had this information too.

In the parking lot behind the building, he selected a likely-looking private car, one that didn't seem to have been driven much lately and, hence, might not be missed too quickly. He hot-wired it, and drove out the gate of the Senior Command compound.

Destination: Virginia Beach.

SEVENTEEN

MARILU BLACK had been the high school and college sweetheart of Roger Black. They were married the week after he received his Bachelor's degree in accounting and finance at Texas Christian University and a week before he joined the Navy. Now she was the wife of Lieutenant (Junior Grade) Roger Black (Supply Corps), USNR, presently Disbursing Officer aboard the U.S.S. *Forrestal.*

He was what they called a "short-timer"; only three months to go on his obligation, and then they could get back to serious living in Graceland, Texas. Home. Where almost everybody they knew went to church; most to the same one—First Southern Baptist. In the beginning, Roger had toyed with the idea of a career in the Navy, but the life wasn't really for either of them.

She was busying herself about their trim development house in a section of Virginia Beach favored by young married officers with children, getting their two—Bobby Joe, two, and Cathee Lee, eight months—ready for a children's party at church. She looked at the kitchen clock when the doorbell rang. It was eight until ten.

She invited the polite Lieutenant Commander in, apologized for the messy house—children, you know—and offered him a cup of coffee. He accepted with a comment about needing it after the previous night's over-indulgence. (Another reason why the Navy life wasn't for either of them: too blessed much overindulgence and too much pressure to join in.)

Marilu answered the stranger's questions politely but firmly. Roger would not consider re-upping for another tour, thank you. Though she smiled sweetly throughout the brief interview, she was adamant: no more Navy for either one of them.

The visitor finally left, but not before going out to his car for a camera, with which he took several color pictures of Marilu and the children. Just by coincidence, he was headed next for Naples and the *Forrestal*, and promised to take them to Roger in person. How thoughtful of him!

"But you hear, Commander, don't try to butter up my Roger so's you can sign him up again."

Commander What's-His-Name allowed as he wouldn't and took his leave.

A little while later, while driving their two-year-old Dodge stationwagon to church, Marilu Black thought to tell Roger about the Commander's visit; then remembered that she'd promised not to so Commander Whatsis could surprise him. He promised he'd do just that the moment he got aboard.

EIGHTEEN

AT JUST that moment, Kolnikov was gunning his "borrowed" car out onto the first stretch of the Cape Charles-Norfolk Bridge Tunnel toward the southern tip of the Delmarva Peninsula, still out of sight over the northern horizon seventeen miles away.

He was elated. Everything so far had gone off like the plot of a cheap adventure novel. Now, all he had to do was change back into civvies at the first gas station on the other side, keep his speed judiciously under the ticket-getting velocities between here and Newark Station, take the next train in to Penn Station, check his bag containing the traveler's checks and his "disguise" in the Baggage Room, then take an untraceable subway ride via the northbound 7th Avenue line to 42nd Street, then the Crosstown Shuttle and the Lexington Avenue line.

And he'd be back into bed with Tina in time for cocktails!

He'd field Roschestvensky's questions later.

NINETEEN

SIMON WAS already in the lobby of Tina's building. He stood up and walked over to Kolnikov the moment he walked in.

"Come with me, Victor."

They walked out together to a black Chevrolet sedan parked along the sidewalk a short way down Fifty-ninth Street.

"Get in the car." Roschestvensky's face was grim. Or was it worried? Kolnikov complied, sliding across to the far side of the back seat. Simon worked his long frame in next to him and closed the door. He turned to Kolnikov.

"All right, Victor—let's have it. Where have you been?"

Kolnikov took his time getting out a cigarette—he offered one to Roschestvensky, who refused it—and lit it. He took two deep, deliberate puffs.

"To the palace to visit the queen."

Roschestvensky bristled, but said nothing. He just continued to bore into Kolnikov with his piercing, gunmetal grey eyes.

"If you must know, I was in Philadelphia. I went to visit the graves of my parents. You remember them? And you can check it with the Yellow Cab records, if you want to."

"You could've done it in a day. Where did you stay overnight?"

"With a friend."

"What friend?"

"None of your goddamned business."

Roschestvensky ignited.

"I've had it with your bullshit, Victor. You're going back."

"No, I'm not!" Victor's eyes were even colder than Roschestvensky's.

"If you try anything, I swear I'll blow you away myself!"

Kolnikov remembered, then, that he thought he had seen—or rather, vaguely sensed—the bulge of a gun under Roschestvensky's coat when they were still in the lobby.

"I wouldn't try that either."

"And why not?"

"Because I also made a stop at the office of an excellent Philadelphia lawyer—the friend I stayed with, incidentally." Kolnikov paused for effect. "I left him a sealed envelope detailing this whole operation—that there *are* moles still operating in the organization, so deeply bored and so high up and for so long that nobody's been able to dig them out; that they managed to frame me and Gruber and Lowell to cover their asses; and that now you people are so afraid of what they've got up their sleeves that you sprung us for bait as a last, desperate measure." Kolnikov paused again. Roschestvensky was sitting transfixed. "And, if he doesn't hear from me—*in person* —in thirty days—and each month thereafter —he's to open it, make copies, and send them to the Times, the Washington Post, Jack

Anderson . . . *and* . . . the National Enquirer!"

Roschestvensky's face was white. "You bastard!"

"I told you, Simon—I'm not going back. I . . ."

Simon had regained his composure and interrupted. "You won't get away with it, Victor. It won't be believed."

Kolnikov grinned and winked theatrically. He was already beginning to look like Uncle Vanya.

"Oh yes it will, Simon. I also had him execute a signed affidavit in the presence of witnesses—and notorized—that I was in his office, yesterday—*in person*. You won't be able to cover that one. And just in case you try, we took my picture in a bank, with a large calendar behind us; and that's notorized too."

Roschestvensky collapsed into the seat.

Kolnikov opened the door on his side and got out. Then he leaned back in and spoke to Roschestvensky, who sat staring dumbly ahead.

"Don't worry, Simon. I won't blow your show and I won't go after Gelman—not yet, anyway. But I'm out and I intend to stay out." Roschestvensky didn't budge.

"I'm sorry, Simon," Kolnikov muttered, and closed the door firmly but gently. Then he strode swiftly back to the lobby.

TWENTY

SUNDAY WAS given over to rest and recreation —called R and R in the service, and known unofficially as I and I for intoxication and intercourse—with Tina. Since it wasn't yet noon, they had indulged in only the first I; on the bed, then on the couch, finally opting for the larger canvas of the floor to frame their sprawling desire. Kolnikov's appetite seemed to grow rather than diminish with each frenzied round. Tina's grew apace; she had forgotten just how good Victor was, and now she was reveling in the delights of rediscovery.

The sun was boring down from zenith when they finally dragged their weary bodies to the shower; even there they couldn't resist a little afterplay under the refreshing cascades.

Then, while Tina concocted them both a large, strength-resuscitating breakfast, Victor slipped out for the Sunday New York Times.

He perused the news indifferently over four extra large eggs, with fat Italian sweet sausages and heaps of jammed toast, then settled into the couch with the rest of the bulky paper. Passing the Travel, Fashion, and Arts and Leisure sections to Tina, who joined him with a sigh of pleasant exhaustion, he took up the Automotive section.

"Planning to buy a car, sweetheart?"

Kolnikov shrugged. "Maybe. When I get some money."

Tina turned back to her reading and was deep into the delights of the Italian Tyrol in the spring when Victor found what he was really looking for. Under "Classic Cars For Sale" there were two separate entries:

ALVIS. 1937 3-ltr. drphd. cp. Needs slt. body wk. & top. Make offer. Eves. aft. 7.

That was Lowell.

MERCEDES-BENZ 1949 170 Sdn. Needs trans. Body minor rust. Make offer. Eves. aft. 7.

And that was Gruber.

Each had followed Kolnikov's longstanding instructions in case they ever got out and had no other means to connect. And both had moved immediately, in time to make the classified deadline for the nearest Sunday out. Good! That meant they'd be off and running long before Roschestvensky would be likely to believe they could make contact, much less plan anything. He'd be caught flat-footed.

Victor memorized the two telephone numbers, then passed on to other entries. He circled several other legitimate entries should Simon's people want to check, which he was certain they would. Later, while Tina was making the first cocktails of the afternoon, he checked the area codes in the telephone directory; he was pleased to find that neither was too far away. Gruber was in Pittsburgh and Lowell in Buffalo, less than a day's trip by bus or car. If they were on the same reporting schedule as Kolnikov was, they'd have time and then some to make the rendezvous.

Afterwards Victor joined Tina in the joys of the first I, alternating through the rest of the afternoon with more of the second. Nine years of sexual drought were fast becoming only a hurtful memory, silted over by the ardent floodtide of Tina.

TWENTY-ONE

A LITTLE before seven, Kolnikov amused his drowsy consort with the suggestion that he slip down to the neighborhood food market for a couple dozen raw oysters.

Chuckling sleepily, she retorted, "Since when do you need those, darling?"

"I don't. I just crave some."

"Pregnant so soon? *Really*, Victor . . ."

"Not pregnant, dear, just hungry for some of the things I missed in there." He waved his thumb vaguely northeast toward New England. "In fact, I think I'll do some shopping around. I'm sure there are lots of things I forgot about in all that time. Do you want anything while I'm there?"

"No, darling," she mumbled digging her tired body deeper under the covers and putting the pillow over her beautifully disheveled hair, "just go easy on the oysters. I'm a bit sore." She let out an exaggerated groan and rolled on her back, her arms outstretched toward Kolnikov. "Come give me one more kiss, darling, and then take your time. I'm taking time out for a nap."

Kolnikov kissed her tenderly, then headed out through the living room to the hall. He considered the fire stairs, then thought better of it, taking the elevator instead. After the long absence on Friday and Saturday, his keepers would be extra alert.

The Gristedes Market on First Avenue just above Fifty-seventh Street was a deprived man's delight. Kolnikov took his time among the rows of gourmet delicacies, selected several long-denied favorites, then was delighted to find that the fresh raw oysters he genuinely hungered for were indeed available. Large, cold, succulent Blue Points. He ordered four dozen, shucked fresh, which amused the jolly, rotund deli manager, who joked about their likely use. Victor cheerfully returned the fishmonger's goodnatured New York banter, debating the truth or untruth of the bland bivalves' efficacy. He paid the cashier and started out of the store.

Then he remembered the hot sauce.

Victor's sudden change of direction outside the door brought him into collision with the man who had been not too far behind him when he walked down from Tina's, and who had entered the store right after he did. He had obviously been rushing to pay for his single purchase and be out so as not to lose Victor. *Damn Roschestvensky!* The man excused himself and left, walking south on the avenue.

Kolnikov found his hot sauce, then crossed the avenue to the west side, stealing a glance southward as he went. He was a tail, all right. Either that, or he liked to windowshop banks.

A little way up the block, Victor ducked into Raimondo's Bar. He had investigated it earlier in the week, and it offered him two advantages at this particular moment: his shadow couldn't follow him in without being even more obvious than before—damned amateur!—and the public phone was in a niche next to the restrooms, back out of sight from the entrance. From behind the small group clustered around the bar, Kolnikov called his drink order over to the bartender, then hastened back to the phone.

Lifting the receiver, he now employed the one really useful thing he had learned in prison—"toning" the Bell System's new touchtone equipment. He had learned it one day from a garrulous phone company installer who no doubt thought that Kolnikov would never have a chance to use it.

Pausing a moment to practice the pitches he intended to use, he then began to whistle a series of notes into the mouthpiece. First a one, then eight hundred, then the number for the National Defense Network's main trunk; then, as soon as he heard it click into line, the area code and number of the second entry in the Times.

It was just seven-thirty when Martin Gruber lifted the receiver at a carefully selected public phone booth in a quiet suburb of Pittsburgh.

Kolnikov began the prerehearsed exchange:

"Are you the man who has the Mercedes-Benz for sale?"

The familiar voice responded. "Yes, but it's a convertible."

Gruber was free to talk, or felt so.

"That's all right, I like them, too." Kolnikov was clean on his end.

Kolnikov continued. "Gruber, I have to talk fast . . ."

The instructions were simple. Get another false identity, two Naval identity cards—active-duty green—and a passport in yet another identity. Buy a complete set of Navy enlisted blues. And be at the Sheraton across from Penn Station in New York by no later than early Tuesday evening. "Phone me from the bar, here's the number . . ." He gave Gruber the number on the phone in front of him. "At precisely twenty-one-hundred." Then Kolnikov gave Gruber the number for Lowell, and told him to relay the same instructions.

Kolnikov hung up the receiver. Less than four minutes had elapsed. There would be no record of the call for Roschestvensky's spooks to trace. As he started back to the bar to collect his drink, Tuesday's date sunk in—April Fool's Day!

In Pittsburgh, Gruber shifted to another phone for the sake of security and called Lowell. The instructions would be simple to follow, though both would have to work fast. Master forgery had been part of the routine training of all three. That very evening, two sailors on liberty would discover that the friendly chap who promised to take them along to a party where there would be "plenty of booze and broads for everybody" was really intent on relieving them of their wallets; a common enough occurrence so that the Navy would make only a routine flap over the lost ID cards. The passports would be equally easy.

Buying the uniforms would be routine. Both Gruber and Lowell had spent time im-

121

personating enlisted men aboard ship as part of ONI's "Operation Queen Bee"—ferreting out homosexuals in the ranks—so playing First Class Petty Officer and Second Class Petty Officer respectively would be a snap. But their specialty designation was unusual —Paymaster. Really curious. What did Victor have up his sleeve?

But they had trusted him as his assistants in ONI Counter-Intelligence, and then for nine years inside.

He must obviously know something. So Paymasters they would become.

TWENTY-TWO

APRIL FOOL'S DAY is small competition for Saint Patrick's Day in New York bars, but there was a much bigger than usual Tuesday-night crowd in Raimondo's.

Tina and Victor had taken the last seat in the far corner, and seemed to be enjoying themselves. Tina was seated on the stool with Victor standing close against her, his fulsome trench coat nearly covering them both. Between sips of their drinks and bits of conversation, they kissed each other again and again; too fervently, it seemed, for the comfort of two single men on the make who were sitting on the other side of the bar. Finally, one called over to Victor.

"I'd sure like to be where you're going tonight."

Kolnikov turned his head and threw him a nod and a knowing, somewhat triumphant—or was it ironic?—smile.

Because Victor was already there. Underneath the cover of his coat and their mutual outward calm, Tina and Victor were luxuriating in a long, slow, excruciatingly delicious fornication. Tina's leg muscles were quivering with the unaccustomed strain of locking them around Victor's from the angle of her perch on the bar stool. She giggled.

"If they only knew!"

"Want to show them?"

"You're a sadistic bastard."

"Am I?" Kolnikov gave her a vicious thrust. Tina shuddered.

"Careful, darling. I told you I can't keep my mouth shut at times like these. Don't push your luck."

"Then what can I push?"

"Me! Me, my horny Russian Teddy Bear." The last thought hit her hard, and she started panting. "Take it . . . easy . . . If I . . . lose my cool . . . we'll . . . get busted."

"With some luck, they might give us a cell together."

Tina laughed. "Don't you ever get enough?"

"Not of you." Tina smiled and closed her eyes. Victor looked at his watch. It was eight-fifty-four. He leaned in and kissed her on the ear. "Are you almost there?"

"Yes, Victor . . . yes . . . but . . . I'm afraid if I . . . come, I'll . . . cry out and give us away."

"Do it anyway," he whispered. "Nobody'll notice; it's too noisy."

"Oh Christ, I wish I had your control. You could've been a Jesuit."

"I'm glad you don't! And I couldn't've been a Jesuit—I'm Orthodox."

Suddenly Tina's hands clamped unto his biceps.

"Oh! Oh, *God*, Victor . . . I'm *doing* it!"

And Victor joined her.

The phone rang. It was barely audible out at the bar. One of the waiters answered, then called out into the crowded room.

"Victor Kolnikov!"

Victor turned his face around toward the

124

waiter, waved to him, and shouted, "That's me—I'm coming."

And Tina exploded in a paroxysm of hysterical laughter.

She had still barely contained herself by the time Kolnikov returned a few minutes later. Most of the bar had grown quiet with curiosity. Kolnikov reassured them.

"Don't worry folks," he bellowed, "just a private joke." Then he turned to Tina, and whispered.

"A *very* private joke." And now, they both laughed, though not as loudly as Tina the first time. Tina was the first to speak.

"Oh, Victor darling, life is really so much fun with you—I love it, and I love you." She hugged and kissed him ardently. Victor pushed her away to arms length, and stared straight into her dark eyes.

"Really? Could you really love only one man?"

"If that one man were you—yes." Then she grew serious. "In fact, Victor, you're the only man of all of them that I ever loved."

Victor hung his head for a long moment, then looked up.

"Then, I want you to do something for me." Tina nodded. "I want you to wait here for two . . . three . . . hours. Then go home and wait for me."

"Wait for you? How long?"

"Not very long, darling. And then we can be together as long as you like."

"Is that a proposal, Victor?"

"Yes. Now will you do it?"

Tina nodded eagerly. Victor wondered whether the tears that had started to dry up weren't seeming to come back into her eyes. He took her face in his hands tenderly and kissed her several times. Yes, she was crying. Then he kissed her once more and walked quickly to the back of the bar near the telephone. He looked back into the crowded room. If there was a tail on him, whoever it was must be outside, because nobody moved.

Then he slipped out through the kitchen and the rear service exit.

TWENTY-THREE

KOLNIKOV SPRINTED out through the alley, then along Fifty-eighth Street to Second Avenue, where he snared a passing cab. At Columbus Circle, he transferred himself to the IRT 7th Avenue line south to Penn Station. There he retrieved his suitcase and threaded his way through the underground concourses to a stairway marked "Penn Sheraton Hotel."

Gruber and Lowell were in a booth near the back of the restaurant. They had ordered dinner and were already eating when Kolnikov joined them. It was just ten o'clock.

"Don't get up," he ordered as he slipped into the seat next to Gruber. Then he ordered a double vodka for himself and fresheners for his two companions from the headwaiter, who had conducted him over.

"Any problems?"

"None at all," Lowell volunteered. "They paid very little attention to us, no apparent tails. The only restriction was that we have to be by the phones at our hotels when they call each morning at zero-eight-hundred." Gruber's nod confirmed this.

"Good. Then we have until eight tomorrow before they start sounding General Quarters —which they will the moment they realize all three of us are over the hill." Both muttered in agreement. Lowell looked worried; he threw down the dregs of his drink and leaned across to Kolnikov.

"Then what happens? Our agreement—at least, *my* agreement with Roschestvensky—was that we weren't to go off on our own show. We aren't even supposed to be together." He looked around, as if expecting at any moment to be seized by someone or something. The youngest of the three by far at thirty-six, he was also the least bold. Unlike Kolnikov and Gruber, who had next to nothing to lose anymore, Jonathan Coolidge Lowell did. A New England Lowell with historically certified roots running all the way back to the Mayflower, with his mother still living and with the world of social privilege into which he was born still there for him should he be cleared, he had the most to gain from the success of Roschestvensky's plan. He had also taken his conviction and disgrace the hardest. Even the prison site—practically in view of the Coolidge-Wentworth Museum, one of that region's many shrines to those hard Yankee Samurai who took Duty, Honor, Country practically with their mother's milk—stood as a constant reproach. Yet he had aged the least during the past nine years (unless one studied his eyes). With his well-kept flaxen hair over large, studious-looking hornrimmed glasses, he still looked like an only slightly overage Choate-Harvard preppie—which he was. He was also more dependent on Kolnikov than the sturdy Gruber. And, Kolnikov suspected, the most completely loyal.

A waiter brought their drinks before Kolnikov could reply. He took a small sip of his and spoke, keeping his voice low, even though none of the booths or tables nearby were occupied and the others were well out of earshot.

"You've still got time to get back before eight if you want out, Jon."

Lowell shook his head. "Not yet, Victor. I want to know what you're up to." He paused to taste his new drink. "Do you know where Gelman and the others are? I take it this has to do with them?"

"No, I don't know where they are."

"Then, how do you expect to find them," Gruber interjected, "with Roschestvensky and half the ONI looking for us and knowing that we're looking for them?"

"We won't be looking for them. We're going to where they're not."

The two looked at each other, puzzled, then at Kolnikov, who slipped his favorite cartoon out of his pocket and spread it on the table as he continued.

"Let's look at the actual situation, gentlemen." Victor held up his left hand and ticked off its fingers with his right. "We're free—or out, rather. But only because nobody has any hard leads—no leads, for that matter. We're out only because Simon's desperate; he has a *hunch* that something's about to go down soon and that, by springing us out at this moment, his action will *somehow* throw a monkey wrench in their plans. And that, *if* he's right, they'll get curious or have to find out what's up, and blow their cover trying. Right?"

129

Kolnikov paused to light a cigarette, then proceeded.

"But if he's wrong. If his timing is off. Or Gelman and company have the sense to sit tight, where are we? Back in the hole, and this time with no chance of ever getting out alive."

Gruber and Lowell agreed; then Gruber spoke up.

"So what do you suggest we do if we don't go after them ourselves?" Kolnikov was waiting for the question.

"I'm not going after Gelman. Frankly, I don't have any faith in Simon's plan—none at all. Gelman's too smart to sucker for a red herring like this; it's almost too obvious—he won't come out."

"Then, why is Simon doing it?" queried Lowell.

"Because he's desperate, he's got nothing left."

Gruber turned to Kolnikov.

"Well then, Victor, if you don't believe Simon's plan can do it, and you don't plan to take out Gelman yourself, what's left?"

"Us." Kolnikov waited for this to register. "We save our own asses, and the hell with the odds of being cleared."

"In other words, we should just run?" asked Lowell. His expression made it plain that he was already regretting the trip from Buffalo.

"Not exactly, Jon. Just running—as you put it—isn't the answer. Even if we took off right now, and with all we know about cover and deception, they'd have us all back in

130

ninety days. For one thing, the case was too spectacular; our faces would be in every two-bit newspaper and magazine and on every television screen in the world. We wouldn't have a chance. No. We're going to run, all right; but we're going to do it right—with a plan and with enough money: first, to assure asylum, and second, to enjoy it—and I mean *enjoy* it."

Gruber grabbed Kolnikov's upraised hand and guided it firmly down onto the table top.

"Back up a minute, Victor. You're suggesting we split—and, I take it, with a *lot* of bread." Gruber held up his hand as he took a swig, then thought before speaking again. "You're talking about asylum, of which there are only two possibilities: that we go over to the other side or we hightail it to Brazil, or perhaps Ireland, where there's no extradition treaty." He stopped again, still signaling for silence. "And of the two, Brazil's more certain. But to stay there, we'd have to have millions . . . not only so we don't get booted out as indigent aliens, but so we can grease the palms we have to grease in order to keep the locals from selling us back to our people for a few hundred grand." Gruber looked from Kolnikov to Lowell and back to Kolnikov. "You couldn't do it! It'd take the biggest heist in history to raise the kind of money we'd need."

"Exactly, Max." Victor gave them both his sliest smile and raised his glass in toast to them before throwing down his drink. Then he turned and bellowed for the waiter, who responded with long-practiced alacrity.

"More drinks. Make them all doubles." Gruber and Lowell sat silent, in thought; Kolnikov let them hang until the drinks arrived and the waiter was back out of hearing range.

"Now, gentlemen. Here's my plan."

Kolnikov tapped the cartoon with his ample finger. Both men grinned, Lowell very nervously.

"As you may or may not know, the average take on a bank robbery is twenty-five hundred dollars. It would take guns, and could get messy. And I figure we'd have to pull off twenty-five hundred of them successfully to get the kind of money I have in mind —or about thirty times as many as John Dillinger." He shook his head. "No. The odds are against us, there."

"Then there's embezzlement. The average embezzler hits the books for fifty thousand. We'd only have to pull a few more than a hundred to make it. But each one could take years, and even three at a time . . . well . . . I figure time's against us. Besides, we couldn't be in position for the *first* one before we'd be taken."

Gruber had been doodling on a cocktail napkin. When Kolnikov paused, he looked up. "According to my fingers, you're thinking somewhere in the vicinity of five to six million, or more. Just where do you expect to knock over that much in cash without a whole goddamned army?"

"Where there's five to seven million sitting right where we can walk in and walk right out with it. Without firing a shot. In fact, without even carrying a gun." Kolnikov spoke slowly, emphasizing each separate word.

Gruber made a face like a man annoyed by a bad joke.

"Oh bullshit, Victor. Stop playing with yourself. Stop dreaming. It's not like you. There's no such thing!"

"There is."

"Where?" Gruber's broad jaw jutted defiantly toward Kolnikov.

"The cash payroll of the *Forrestal*—in Naples."

Gruber's jaw dropped. Lowell sat bolt upright. He had looked uncomfortable until now. Now his eyes flickered about as if he thought the Recording Angel were listening nearby. Kolnikov stood up.

"Excuse me, gentlemen. I have to visit the head."

TWENTY-FOUR

KOLNIKOV TOOK his time. Gruber and Lowell were huddled over the table arguing in whispers when he returned. They both stopped and regarded Victor with a mixture of puzzled amusement as he slid back into the booth. Gruber spoke first.

"Okay, Victor. We figure we might as well hear the rest of the story. The money's there, all right. But how do you propose getting it off with an aircraft carrier and half the Sixth Fleet around it?"

Kolnikov pulled a leather passport case from an inside pocket and opened it. He laid several color snapshots on the table. One showed a youngish blonde, pretty but plain and already frumpish in a rural sort of way. She held a baby in one arm; a boy clung to her other hand. Two showed the little boy only—one with him pushing a musical roll-toy on the lawn, the other with him astride a plastic rocking horse. Another showed Kolnikov holding both children.

"Lieutenant JG Roger Black, Supply Corps, is the *Forrestal*'s Disbursing Officer. He's going to *give* us the money. In fact, he's even going to help us carry it ashore."

Lowell picked up the photographs and examined them. Kolnikov pointed to the woman.

"Marilu Black is his wife. Those are his children."

Gruber let out a low whistle. "You're serious. You're actually going to *do* it!" His head gave a quick shake as if he were mentally pinching himself.

"Yes, Max, I am. And I think you know exactly how."

Gruber nodded. "That's why the Paymaster designations. You're planning to pull a phony *surprise audit!*" His eyes glinted brighter as each layer of understanding peeled itself back in his head. "And you'll be . . ."

"Lieutenant Commander Vasyli M. Kolchov, Supply Corps, Officer-in-Charge of the audit team. And you'll be my assistants."

"Christ, Jon . . . he can do it!"

Lowell looked up at Gruber as if shaken from a dream. "Do what? I've never been on a carrier."

"He can walk off with the whole bundle. He simply goes onboard with us and says he's there to conduct a surprise audit of the Disbursing Officer's funds—it's done all the time, just like a surprise bank audit. And then, he blackmails the Disbursing Officer into handing over the money . . . that *is* what the pictures are for, aren't they, Victor?"

"Exactly. And we'll be in Rio de Janeiro less than twenty-four hours later. With at least two million apiece—enough to buy half the broads on Ipenema Beach and all the booze in the Copacabana a thousand times over. Interested?"

Gruber suddenly grew serious. "What if it doesn't work? What if we get caught?"

"Then we go back to Portsmouth, just like we will if Simon doesn't pull a miracle out of his ass."

"You don't have too much faith in Roschestvensky's plan, do you?"

"Not at all, Max. It's a total long shot. And if it does work, where are we? After all the publicity, the sensational coverage in the press . . . after nine years of burying three innocent men up there . . . then having to admit they were dead wrong . . . that there's been a mole operation running loose in ONI for . . . how long? . . . maybe twenty years? They couldn't turn around and vindicate us publically. Jesus, it'd bring down the government."

"So what would they do?"

"At best, they'd terminate Gelman and his crew—if they didn't exchange them—all hush-hush. Then, they'd pull some bureaucratic bullshit like pardoning us—*if* we agreed to go along with the coverup. We'll never get it all back."

"You've got it all figured out, don't you, Victor?"

"I had lots of time."

"And how do you figure the odds on heisting the *Forrestal*?"

"No less than fifty-fifty. Probably better. It's the old ploy of the totally inconceivable, like Skorczeny's capture of Horthy. Remember that one?"

Gruber shook his head.

"Otto Skorczeny was Hitler's chief of Commandos. When the Russians reached the Hungarian border, the Hungarians started getting shaky, including Admiral Horthy. So, for insurance, Hitler wanted to have Horthy in Berlin where he couldn't pull any deals, such as surrendering or even going over to the other side. He invited him to a conference in Berlin. But Horthy wasn't crazy. He holed himself up in Buda Castle and surrounded it with the entire crack Royal Division.

"Hitler gave Skorczeny the job of capturing Horthy. But how? He couldn't mount one of his usual lightning attacks—not on a supposed ally—and not against a whole division.

"So you know what he did, Max? He assembled a *single company* of Waffen SS in full parade dress, with their regimental band and a couple of open cars, at six A.M. on a Sunday morning, at the far end of Pest. Then, he *paraded* them—flags flying, band playing —down the main boulevard of Pest to the bridge over the Danube. Crossed to the Buda side, then up the main boulevard of Buda, *right up and into Buda Castle!* The Hungarians opened all the road blocks and gates and saluted them through. When Skorczeny's car got inside, he and two others dashed up to Horthy's apartment, went into his bedroom, woke him up, pointed a pistol at his head, and said, 'Come with me.' It was the slickest piece of work since the Trojan Horse."

"I get your point."

Max Gruber was getting Kolnikov's point every step of the way; Victor expected him to. Only four years younger, Maximillion Frederic Gruber had been Victor's chief assistant for three years before Gelman turned the tables on them. And, if possible, he hated Gelman even more than Kolnikov did, and for more reasons. A product of working-class Germans who had settled in Milwaukee, he was raised by parents who sincerely wanted to believe that Jesus Christ was not a Jew. His father and both uncles belonged to the Bund; his mother, aunts, and older sister were fervent auxiliaries. The war changed only some of their beliefs, though both his father and one uncle died heroes in it. A graduate of Northwestern University in Criminology and Psychology, he was a natural for Intelligence; his family's former allegiances didn't weigh too heavily against him because of his youth at the time—he was only three when the war started—and because the evils of Nazism had taken a far back seat by the end of the anti-Communist Fifties. A star athlete, with immense strength on a large frame and with an utterly ruthless turn of mind, he was one of the department's "hard" men. Unlike Lowell, their studious and patient detail man, Gruber was a hunter-killer. He was the first to suspect Gelman and his team, if only because he automatically hated and distrusted Gelman from the moment they met. And he pursued him with the monomaniacal zeal of the Grand Inquisitor.

Max Gruber was the epitome of the stereo-type Teuton, as classically Germanic as Lowell was Anglo-WASP. Even in U.S. Navy blues he managed to look like something straight off an S.S. recruiting poster. Kolnikov often thought that, had Max Gruber been born a few years sooner and on the other side, he would have still wound up in prison —if not on an Allied gallows.

Kolnikov very much wanted Gruber for the heist. He wanted his ice-cold nerves and unshakeable guts—he had adjusted first and best to imprisonment; Lowell had taken it the hardest. If he could have only one, he preferred Gruber.

Now he asked him.

"What about it, Max? Are you for it?"

"Are you, Victor?"

"I'm going—with or without either or both of you. So what is it?"

Gruber rubbed his chin pensively for several moments, then looked from Lowell to Kolnikov. "I think you're right about the situation. And I believe we could pull off the heist . . . and probably get away with it. But there's still two questions. What happens to Roschestvensky? And what about Gelman?"

Kolnikov was ready for both.

"I'm sorry about Simon—very sorry. But we were innocent, Max, and it didn't save us from what happened. I figure we have an even slimmer chance than we had at the court-martial, and I'm not about to gamble the rest of my life on odds like that. I swore— I warned Simon—that I'd never go back in there alive. And I won't. True, there's some risk in this heist, but I figure it's the best way to insure my freedom."

"And what about Gelman?"

139

A smile slowly spread across Kolnikov's face until he seemed to be nothing but mouth and glittering eyes.

"I plan to use some of my share of the loot to buy a first-class contract on all three—Gelman, Horn, and Stoddard. Would you like to contribute to the fund?"

"I'm in!"

Kolnikov raised his glass to Gruber, who also lifted his.

"*Nastrovya!*"

"*Prosit!*"

They both turned to Lowell, who had been hunched into the corner of his seat as if in another world. Gruber challenged him first.

"What about you, Jon? Would you like to join us in retirement in sunny Rio instead of that Naval Rathole-By-The-Sea?"

Lowell squirmed. He fidgeted. Then took command of his obviously conflicting feelings and looked up.

"I don't think so, Max. I'd rather take my chances here."

"What chances, Jon? You heard what Victor said. We're all dead ducks if we stay—no matter which way it goes. So why not go along?"

Lowell shook his head. Kolnikov joined in.

"Jon. If it's the heist that bothers you, then you don't have to be part of it. Come along with us. I'll share my portion with you. And you can maybe continue a legal fight from Brazil. God knows, none of us have been permitted to fight. They buried us up there and threw the keys away. They gave us no chance, no communication. No nothing. If you're free, the heist will put us all back in the world news. We could even blow the story about Roschestvensky's attempt to smoke the real guilty ones out, and the publicity just might shake the truth loose. Take a chance. Come with us."

Lowell continued to shake his head. He closed his eyes as if trying to blot out the idea —or was it the temptation? Gruber leaned over and started to speak. Kolnikov put his hand against his shoulder and urged him silently back in his seat. Then Victor sat back and spoke quietly to Lowell.

"You don't have to do it if you don't want to, Jon." He paused, the younger man brightened. "Just one thing. If you don't go, you don't blow the whistle on us. Agreed?"

"Agreed. I won't, Victor—I promise."

"Fair enough, Jon. Now, we had all better get going. You'll just about make it back. Can you, Jon? Good."

Kolnikov stood up first, and turned back to Gruber.

"And we've got to make tracks too."

"So soon? When do we leave . . . how . . ."

Kolnikov retrieved the photos from the table. He slipped them back into the passport case, and pulled out three red, white, and green folders.

"Three paid and confirmed reservations on the one A.M. Alitalia New York-to-Rome flight tonight, Max."

Gruber chuckled ironically.

"Pretty confident, weren't you, Victor?"

"One out of two. That's fifty-fifty odds— and if my luck holds, we'll make it."

They both shook hands with Lowell, who hurried out through the lobby. Just before he disappeared through the door, Gruber turned to Kolnikov.

"Do you think it's safe to leave him out of it? He might get cold feet and talk. Or make a deal. Victor . . . I think we'd be safer if he couldn't . . . if . . . I took him out?"

Kolnikov enveloped Gruber's shoulder in a powerful, one-armed bear hug.

"If it were you instead of him, Max, I might —just might—consider it."

TWENTY-FIVE

THE CLOCK behind the bar in the darkened Sky Lounge indicated five minutes after twelve when the bartender served Kolnikov and Gruber their second round of drinks.

Checked in and just waiting for the boarding call, they were avoiding the public reception area with its potential for unwanted chance encounters.

Someone sat down next to Kolnikov.

"You didn't cash in that third ticket, did you, Victor?"

"No, I didn't," replied Kolnikov without taking his eyes off the clock in front of them. "What made you change your mind?"

"A bird in the hand started whispering in my ear."

TWENTY-SIX

"SEE NAPLES and die."

The ancient Romans meant it as a compliment. To the American sailors who have to suffer duty or liberty there—to most mariners, in fact—the phrase carries a different meaning. Poverty. Squalor. Disease. Dysentery, cholera, even plague. Dingy bars with watered booze and scruffy whores who can clap you as fast as look at you. Syphilis. Short change. Thieving taxi drivers and pickpockets to relieve you of the rest. And local cops who throw *you* in jail if you complain.

Even the native Neopolitans call it "the crookedest city in the World." *Proudly!*

In Rome in the north, the Italians claim: *a Napoli comincia l'Africa.* "Africa begins at Naples." (Though some Londoners insist that the northern terminus of the Dark Continent is really Calais.) In a country that spawned more beautiful, interesting, delightful cities than any other in Europe, Naples stands apart. Like Rolls-Royce, but with the opposite meaning, one speaks of "the Naples" of other countries. Hamburg. Marseilles. Cork. Liverpool.

An anonymous eighteenth-century traveler summed it up:

"Rome is Eternal—Naples, Infernal."

The *rapido* from Rome swung briefly west along the coast on its final leg before plunging into the long tunnel that ends in Mergelina Station, revealing an almost unbroken panorama of sand and sea glistening in the late afternoon sun. Its clean beauty here belied the pandemic miasma that lay just south of the massive mountain ridge which juts out into the Mediterranean, containing Naples and mercifully blotting out its prospect from the north.

Kolnikov, Gruber, and Lowell had all been there before; only business or duty could've brought them back. They had managed to grab three of the five seats in the forward observation section of the first car just in front of the engineer's domed cab on top. From there, they shared his view as the train silently gobbled up the track ahead at over 100 kilometers per hour. For Kolnikov, a train buff, it was his favorite place on one of his very favorite trains. They were alone save for a fat Italian matron with her two small children who were noisily playing engineer; Kolnikov delighted them from time to time by joining in.

"You must really like children," observed Lowell.

"Yes I do. And when this job's over, I'm going to settle down with a great big, brawling, bawling brood of my own."

"Something from Ipenema?"

"Perhaps. Perhaps not." Lowell's question made him think of Tina. A feeling of longing grew in him. He really was in love with her! Too bad she couldn't have come along. But that would've been fatal; even if she could have given them the slip in New York, she'd simply draw too much attention in the Land of Bottom-Pinchers. Kolnikov gave a long sigh. He would just have to play the Jesuit until she could come to him safely. Like that goddamn prison again. He sighed.

"Anything the matter?" Gruber asked.

"Nothing. Just thinking."

"You aren't getting cold feet, are you, Victor?"

"No. I was just thinking about my mother and father." Gruber knew of Tina, but Kolnikov wasn't sharing.

One of the children said something to their mother in Italian. She got up and led them back through the main section of the car to the door marked *gabinetto*. Gruber took the opportunity to ask Kolnikov a question that had been eating at him since soon after the train had left Rome.

"Do you think this situation in Turkey will upset things?" he asked, indicating the copy of the *Rome Daily American* on the seat beside Kolnikov.

"Possibly. But most likely in our favor."

Gruber picked up the newspaper and scanned the lead story. "How so, Victor?"

"Well, the story says that Carrier Division Four has been *alerted* to sail to the trouble area. That indicates that the *Forrestal* is still in her usual operating area on this side of Italy. And, if she's ordered around under any but emergency orders, she'll stop first in Naples to top off supplies—especially money." Kolnikov rubbed his thumb and forefinger together as he flashed a hungry smile.

"What if she's already there?"

"Then we analyze the situation and decide what to do. If she's already there—which I doubt, as the paper would have said so if she were—she may already have replenished her cash. We'll have to find out, if we can—how I don't know. We may just have to go in and take our chances. There'll still be at least two million aboard."

"But just this past Monday was payday."

"All the more reason why they'll have to redraw before they leave."

Lowell, who up to now had seemed mesmerized by the scene which kept rushing at them from ahead, spoke up.

"What if she doesn't come in? What if she's ordered straight around? What if she stays there for weeks . . . or a couple of months?"

"Then we have two choices. We can follow her to Piraeus and hope we can carry it off there." He shook his head. "But I don't like it. There's no direct air service to Brazil from Athens; getting out would mean a plane change—and Customs—at either Rome or Lisbon. The plan calls for direct flight from Rome to Rio; anything else increases the risk." He paused to light a cigarette. "No, Jon. If we miss them, we'll have to wait it out here, for as long as it takes."

"Can we?"

"We have no other choice, Jon. We don't have the money to split, we already know that. But we do have the money to lay low and wait. That's why we're going direct to Capri if the *Forrestal* isn't there when we get there. I chose it because it's the perfect place

147

from which to monitor the situation. We'll know the minute she steams into the Gulf of Naples—you won't miss her! And by hydrofoil we can be on the quay in Naples before she can anchor and send her first boats in."

"Why not just stay in Naples?"

"You should know that, Jon," Gruber chimed in irritably, as if speaking to a child.

"But after nine years, Max?"

"After nine years. Yes, there's been probably a seventy or eighty percent turnover in personnel, but we can't take a chance in a place like Naples . . . crawling with Navy. It'd take only one wrong encounter to blow us all out of the water. Right, Victor?"

"Right. Whereas it's still off-season in Capri and will be until mid-May. Even then, our chances are still better there."

Lowell still wasn't satisfied. "What about Roschestvensky and the rest? What about the publicity when it finally hits the fan about our disappearance?"

"I don't think it will hit the fan—not for a while, at least. If I know Simon, he'll play this ball where it lays and still try to salvage his operation. He has to if he wants to save his own ass. As for looking for us . . . every mother's son of 'em will be looking for us in Washington . . . or perhaps, Norfolk . . . wherever Gelman and his crew are. *Not* on the beautiful Isle of Capri!"

The woman returned with her children, and conversation ceased.

A few minutes later, all six watched the black mouth of the Mergelina Tunnel fly at them like the entrance of a hungry tomb.

TWENTY-SEVEN

FROM FAR enough out in the Gulf, Naples *is* beautiful, at least once a day—when the last flash of the late afternoon sun strikes the wide arc of mountains which embrace the entire region and turns them a stark, bright umber gold. From the Sorrentine Peninsula on the south to far Ischia in the north, everything—brown hills, green olive groves, now-impotent Vesuvius, the dingy *Castello*, even grimy factory chimneys—comes aglow with brilliant antique hues under a deep cobalt sky. Even the oil slicks, which can be found very far out—dirty gray at noon—shimmer with the convoluting colors of a psychedelic dream. It's as if—once a day—the ancient gods forgive.

The three men stood relaxed over the taffrail of the old, rusted steam ferry *Stella di Capri* as she plodded patiently westward toward her namesake island, a black plume of coal smoke from her venerable engines the sole blot against the cloudless sky. A long, low swell from northwest rolled her gently, evenly, like a cradle.

Neither man spoke. Like creatures of darkness suddenly in the sun, they stood transfixed, dazzled by the unaccustomed brightness of an alien—or forgotten—world.

The roll of the ship felt good to Victor. Though more deskbound than deckbound, like most Intelligence officers, he had much more time at sea than Gruber. And Lowell had none, having been commissioned for only three years when he was snared with the other two in Gelman's trap. It was Victor who had insisted on the *Stella di Capri* over the much faster hydrofoil, giving the reason that, being cheaper, it was used almost exclusively by the natives and hence was safer for them. But his real reason was, frankly, just to enjoy the feel of a real ship again, even if it were only this old scow.

A stray patch of offal bobbed past. Gruber broke the silence.

"Christ! All the way out here!"

"Maybe that's from the ship's head," suggested Kolnikov.

"Then I'd hate t'see the ass all that came from," Gruber observed, spitting after it.

As if broken by Gruber's coarse observation, the spell vanished swiftly from the surrounding land. And, deprived of its warming fire, the air chilled almost as quickly. Lowell spoke up as he adjusted the collar of his jacket close about his neck.

"You know, Naples reminds me of the story they tell in New York about the Englishman who, having taken the Circle Line boat tour around Manhattan, suggested that New Yorkers did only three things: defecate, fornicate, and eat oranges."

"Well, in Naples," added Gruber, "they do it in the fucking streets."

The ship passed now into the long shadows cast by the mountainous island, and a few minutes later bumped and squeaked gently against the oft-battered and tattering hemp fenders along the high stone jetty of the lower harbor.

Disembarking a few moments later, they took the modern *funiculare* to the main town, fourteen hundred feet up the mountainside, leaving the long, slow donkey ride for *i turisti*.

The tiny, bijou-like Piazetta was crowded with people, though few looked like tourists. It was Easter Week—*Pasqua*—and the inhabitants were busy preparing for the long period of *feste*—Maundy Thursday, the somber Good Friday, and the joyous Easter Sunday. Intricately embroidered banners, bright bunting, and streamers hung from every available balcony and wall. A two-story-high Madonna and a bigger-than-life-size crucifix reposed on either side of the ornately carved wood doors of the modest tenth-century brown brick church. Its bells were chiming Vespers when the three stepped off the cable car.

"Follow me," Victor commanded quietly, and led the other two as they snaked their way slowly through the crush of people and cafe tables so closely placed together that there was scarcely room for movement. Maneuvering erratically, they made their way more or less diagonally across the square to a low, narrow alley at the far corner. Now away from the packed piazza, they moved more freely, though still carefully, over the alley's irregular stone surface.

A little further on, on the right, Victor took a narrow dirt path which ran steeply up between stone walls on the left and a high hedge on the right. Striding up the incline, they could see nothing in the gloom now. Victor was climbing like one of the mountain goats from which the island got its name. After what seemed three quarters of a mile, they mounted a half-hidden stairway on the left and issued out onto a gently sloping veranda. A little off to one side, half hidden by huge trees, a modest three-story hotel overlooked the entire gulf, now strung with a chain of twinkling lights about its broad, sweeping perimeter.

The Villa Bardi was built in the Twenties, during the first modern tourist boom on the island, and had managed to retain the ambiance of its era. The grand piano in its tastefully understated salon proclaimed its total separation—in time and mood—from the more frenetic establishments down by the town. It catered exclusively to a genteel clientele—mostly Italians and a few others fortunate to know about it. Typically, the rates were a fraction of those charged the foreigners elsewhere.

None of the staff spoke English, or admitted to it. So, while the Gruber and Lowell admired the furnishings, Kolnikov parlayed with the concierge in what he knew of the local tongue.

Finally, the concierge tapped the bell on his desk and a primly starched maid came out and gathered their bags. As he led them up the graceful, curved staircase to the floors above, Kolnikov explained:

"We're in luck. I had forgotten about

Easter, but it seems that Easter's a big family holiday here. So they're actually fairly empty, except for some Germans and Scandinavians who come here nearly every year."

They climbed to the top floor, where their host ushered them into two rooms, each with a spacious, arbored balcony almost as large as the rooms themselves. Gruber and Lowell gathered in Kolnikov's room while the maid distributed the bags and fussed the bedcovers and pillows into shape. The concierge handed Victor the keys and before leaving, asked, *"Vuole qualcosa di bere? O mangiare?"* Gruber and Lowell picked out *vino roso* and the universally familiar *uisgue* from Victor's haltingly detailed reply.

Shortly after, they were relaxing on white wicker chairs and a chaise-longue beside white wicker tables which supported a formidable carafe of red wine, a bottle of Ballantine's scotch, and the remains of three huge, delicious meals of unfamiliar delicacies.

Gruber was sitting angled back on a chair; his large, stockinged feet were perched on the stone lip of the balcony. A half-full glass of neat scotch was making frequent trips to his lips.

"This is the *life*, Victor! How did you know about this place?"

"When I was an Ensign on assignment to COMSOUTH Headquarters. A girl I met out here introduced me to it; used to come here as often as I could get away."

"Y'know, Victor," pondered Gruber, "maybe we should hole up here after the job."

154

"I'd love to, but we'd never make it. I did have my chance, though—once. The girl who brought me here was the granddaughter of a South American dictator . . . had more millions of her own than the *Forrestal* . . . a villa in Rome, a chauffered Cadillac . . . the works . . . and she wanted to marry me."

"Why didn't you?"

"I was young and foolish."

"You'd've saved yourself a lot of trouble."

"Don't remind me." Victor threw down the rest of his wine, then filled another glass with straight whiskey. Gruber turned his head to look at Kolnikov and noticed Lowell; he was fast asleep on the chaise-longue.

"He's a cool one, Victor."

"Probably the wine and the flight."

Gruber lifted his feet off the ledge and swung around to face Kolnikov.

"So what do we do now?"

"We sit tight. Here. Tomorrow, I'll go down into town and nose around the bars to see who knows when the *Forrestal*'s due in."

"Will they know, all the way out here?"

Kolnikov nodded confidently. "As soon as they get the word over in Naples, they'll know it out here."

Gruber gave Victor an understanding glance. The biggest fiction in the world is the so-called "security" of ship movements. Though classified Confidential, and sometimes Secret, their schedule is a wide-open book in any dive in any liberty port. In fact, the only thing all the hush-hush does is make it difficult for the people who should know. Call up the base and ask when a ship's due in, and

155

you get the runaround about "Classified" information. So the experienced hand doesn't bother. One simply asks the bar girls.

Kolnikov sat silently musing over his drink. Something he thought made him smile.

Perhaps, if Hitler had been a barfly instead of a teetotaler, the Germans would've been ready and waiting the morning we landed at Normandy!

TWENTY-EIGHT

THE SUN was already high when Kolnikov shook Gruber out of a deep sleep and into a monumental hangover.

"General Quarters, Max. Hit the deck!" Kolnikov ordered as he shook the groggy blond awake.

"What for, Victor? We just . . . o-o-o-o-o-h . . . oh Christ! My fuckin' head!" Gruber sat up, then lay back holding his cranium as if trying to keep it from slitting any further open.

"She's coming in. This afternoon."

"How do you know?"

"Down at the taverna in the Piazza. The bartender told me." Gruber struggled up as Victor rattled off the details. "Seems she wasn't due until the tenth. But they've moved it up to today. She'll be in this afternoon, and move out as soon as she can get loaded up with extra supplies—probably Monday. The bartender heard it from his sister; her husband works on the Navy dock and he's pissed—everybody's pissed—because they've gotta work over Good Friday and Easter."

Gruber had shaken Lowell awake, and was pouring himself a hair of the dog, though he diluted it with some water from the pitcher on the dresser. "So what's our schedule now?"

Kolnikov also decided on a short one from the bottle, and poured as he talked.

"We have to get it to town and get set up before her boats hit the beach."

"Why so fast?"

"Because—since this is obviously an emergency provisioning, they'll accelerate everything. And in that case, they may have already radioed ahead for a team from COMSOUTH Disbursing to meet them at the dock. Or COMSOUTH might have already suggested it; with Good Friday coming up, they may want to get the transfer over with this afternoon so they won't get their liberty cut short tomorrow." Kolnikov paced back and forth as he talked, occasionally stopping to fix some point or another in his head. "If we hurry, Max, we'll make it. Where's Jon?"

Lowell had gone into the bathroom. Now he returned. Kolnikov noted that he looked ridiculously skinny in just his skivvie shorts.

"What's going on?"

"We'll tell you on the way. Just hurry up and get dressed. We're moving out."

"So soon? I was sort of looking forward to spending the weekend here on the island. With Easter and all, it looked like it'd be loads of fun." He looked genuinely disappointed.

"Don't sweat it, Jon. Carnival in Rio will make this look like the Ladies' Auxiliary annual tea. Take my word for it."

TWENTY-NINE

THEY WERE just in time. As the one-thirty hydrofoil sped clear of the island on its return trip to Naples, the fast-receding cliffs unveiled the vast, behemoth bulk of the U.S.S. *Forrestal* steaming majestically into the gulf from northwest. Five destroyers, looking like minnows following a whale, fanned out in a semicircle behind her.

Kolnikov, with Gruber and Lowell next to him, watched the stately procession from the open afterdeck of the racing *aliscafo*. The whine of her turbines combined with the rushing wind to keep their conversation private from the others aboard.

"She's at Combat Readiness Condition *Yellow*," observed Kolnikov.

"How can you tell?" queried Lowell, squinting as if to uncover what the older man saw. Kolnikov drew his right hand out of his coat pocket and began pointing as he spoke.

"The destroyers, for one thing. They're in Anti-Submarine Screen astern; SOP for entering harbor under readiness conditions. Otherwise, they could've been strung out in some other formation. My guess is they won't go alongside the quay in the harbor as they usually do, but'll anchor out around her so they can get underway immediately if they have to.

"Then there's the carrier herself. See those

planes on her flight deck?" Lowell nodded. "They're not spotted along the edges of the deck like they would be normally." Kolnikov waved his pointing finger to encompass the whole ship, then aimed it at one spot. "Instead, they're lined up on the Cats, one behind the other. The lead ones are already spotted and hooked up ready to launch. All they have to do is put the crews in 'em, start 'em up, and push the button . . . then, one right after the other—wham, wham, wham." He dropped his arms. "And if my guess is right, the crews are at full readiness too, suited up, briefed, and just loafing around the Ready Rooms waiting for the signal."

"Is it that serious?" Lowell looked worried.

"They know something we don't, Jon. See those bombs slung under those planes? Well, I can't be sure from this distance, but their shape isn't conventional; I'd guess them for nukes."

"Nukes?" Gruber now joined Lowell in scrutinizing the giant ship. "Come *on*, Victor!"

"Look for yourself, Max. They're blunt and fat, not aerodynamic like ordinary bombs; and there's only one under each of the smaller planes—and no secondary armament. They're nukes, Max. I've seen them like that once before—during the Cuban Missile Crisis."

Lowell pointed. "Those men up there around the planes, are those guns they're carrying?"

Kolnikov leaned as far aft as he could and squinted. "Marines! They've got Marine sentries around those planes!" He stood back and nodded slowly, with complete confidence in what he said next.

"No doubt about it, gentlemen. Every one of those planes is armed for a nuclear strike."

"But why?"

"That's what I'd like to know. And I'm going to try to find out as soon as we get ashore."

At over fifty knots, the hydrofoil was fast pulling away from the naval formation behind them. About the only thing still clearly distinguishable was the huge 59 blazoned on the carrier's superstructure. Kolnikov turned around and sat down in the stern bench; the other two did likewise, one on either side.

"What does this mean for us, Victor?"

Kolnikov thought for several minutes before replying.

"Well, obviously security will be a little tighter. We may have to show ID and all that, but that's no problem. On the other hand, they'll be too busy with everything they've got to get done to pay too much attention to us; that'll make our job easier. Also, they'll restrict liberty—or have no liberty call at all, most likely. That means less risk of our being recognized by somebody on the beach." Victor rubbed his chin pensively. "Actually, the only thing that could screw us would be if they get emergency orders to up anchor and get underway before we can do our bit."

"Do you think they will?"

Kolnikov turned his palms up. "Who

knows? If they do, we go back to Capri for the rest of our vacation and hope they don't stay away too long."

Lowell suddenly thought of something; he almost jumped in his seat.

"Victor, what if they don't anchor at all? If they're standing by like you say they are, will they anchor where they can't launch their planes?"

"But they *can* launch, Jon."

"They *can*?" Lowell frowned disbelievingly.

"They can. It's a bit hairy, but they can." Kolnikov looked around at the sea. The *Stella di Capri* was lumbering past them to the south, playing tortoise to their hare. Victor checked the drift of her smoke. "See that smoke, Jon? It's drifting off to the southwest. Wind's northwesterly—from the direction of the main channel. Fifteen minutes after they drop the hook, she'll be pointed straight back out the way she came in—and into the wind. And even with no wind, those catapults can do it; they have a terminal velocity of a hundred fifty-five knots." Kolnikov's arm now swept from an imaginary anchorage point to the carrier's present position. "If she has to launch in emergency, she'll just start firing off her planes immediately, slip her anchor chain, and head right out to sea, firing the Cats as she goes. They'll all be off before she's even out of the gulf."

"My God!" Lowell looked stunned. Even Gruber was impressed.

The sudden silence from the turbines, followed by the whack-whack of the hydrofoil's hull hitting the water as its foils subsided back into the waves announced their imminent arrival at the mouth of the Inner Harbor.

The U.S.S. *Forrestal* Heist was about to shift into high gear.

THIRTY

THE HOTEL Londra. The only thing English about it is the name; like most things in Naples, everything else gains weight in translation. An overstated Baroque-Revival pile from the latter half of the last century, it is nevertheless commodious and comfortable. Like a Baroque woman.

Kolnikov engaged a room large enough to accommodate all three. That way they would risk the fewest comings and goings in the hallways. The Londra was the favorite hotel and gathering place for Navy people on the beach. The room had another advantage. It was on the second floor front, which enabled them to keep an eye on the main Navy pier, a block west at the foot of Piazza Municipio. A bribe in the right hand had bumped someone arriving later with a reservation. Ah, *la bella Napoli!*

Kolnikov surveyed the port from the ornately balustraded balcony while Gruber and Lowell stayed just behind him, out of sight from the Piazza.

"We won't be able to do it from here. There's too much activity. We'd need glasses, and we couldn't use them from inside the room. Too risky. We'll have to get closer. Let's go." He turned and charged out of the room with the others in close formation behind him.

As they reached the sidewalk outside and turned westward to the port, Kolnikov commented angrily on the crowded lobby. "I forgot about the *seagulls*. We'll have to be in and out of the lobby as fast as possible."

Lowell turned to Kolnikov. "Seagulls?"

"Wives of officers on the ships who come over during deployment and follow the ships from port to port, sort of legally sanctioned camp-followers. Most of them I'm not worried about, the younger wives. But some of the wives of senior officers might recognize me."

"Did you see anyone you know?"

"I tried not to."

They had reached the port area. Kolnikov led them over boldly to the high cyclone fence separating the sidewalk from the quay. They were about fifty yards south of the gate, away from most of its bustle. The *Forrestal* could be seen, anchored as Victor said she would be with her flat, chisel-like bow pointed out to sea. The destroyers positioned around her like workers around a queen bee.

The first open motor launches were just making the pier to the accompaniment of shouted orders from those whose job it apparently was to transfer stores onto them. Several mountain ranges of boxes and crates were already in position, and trucks with more were pouring into the gate almost every minute.

"I'd hate to be the sailor who fell in that!" remarked Lowell, pointing at the thick morass on the inner harbor, a sluggishly undulating mosaic of garbage, trash, offal, and other indefinable things in a *pot de feu* of what passed for crankcase oil.

"Take a second look," chuckled Gruber. "Some of those big lumps in there *are* sailors. When you fall in here, they don't bother to fish you out."

An officers' launch rounded the lighthouse. Kolnikov instinctively recoiled from the fence and led them back across the busy street to the corner cafe. Selecting a table, they sat.

"We'll have to cover it from here," Kolnikov began. "I don't want to, but there's no other way."

A waiter arrived, took their orders, and left. Victor continued. "We'll have to mount watch today until eighteen-hundred, then each day until sixteen- or seventeen-hundred. I don't think they'll make the transfer after that." He turned his head and surveyed the intersection. "We'll have to alternate places between here, over on the other corner, and from those two up the street. We can't stay in any one place too long. We'll also need newspapers and such to keep us looking occupied." He turned to Lowell. "That big newsstand we passed on the way down?" Lowell nodded. "I'll get you a book—something fat—you're the only one of us who won't look phony with a book."

Gruber interrupted. "What if we pick up a girl or two?"

"If you can work it, Max, all the more power to you."

"Do I get to screw her when I'm off watch?"

"If you can. But do it where I can reach you. And don't take a chance on anything that'll get you in trouble, or rolled."

Their drinks came. Kolnikov bolted his.

"Okay. I'm leaving for awhile. You two know what to look for?"

"An officer, armed, with two or three enlisted men—all carrying bags—and guarded by Marines." Lowell repeated the description Victor had burned into their heads.

"And remember—don't confuse that with a registered publications draw. They'll be armed, but no Marines with machineguns. Get it?" Both men assented. Kolnikov rose and made his way quickly back up the Piazza.

Several blocks further up, he found the offices of Autonoleggio Hertz directly adjacent to the Italian State Tourist Office (commonly pronounced "Cheat" after its initials, CIT—which Victor always thought a piece of poetic justice).

Taking out his wallet, Kolnikov flashed his ID at the pretty girl behind the counter. "I'm Lieutenant Commander Kolchov and I need to rent a car."

"Do you have a reimbursement order, *signore commandante?*"

"No."

"Oh, then this is personal? Do you have a credit card?"

"No, this is official, but it's an emergency. I need it right away." He produced the phony set of audit orders he had prepared, just in case he was questioned by someone aboard the *Forrestal*.

"Then, *signore*, we will need a two-hundred-dollar deposit, plus the insurance deposit—in advance."

"Fair enough." He produced two of his traveler's checks as the girl busied about the forms.

"How long will you need it?"

"About five days."

"Will you return it here?"

"No—in Rome—at Fiumicino . . . er . . . Leonardo da Vinci Airport."

The girl flashed him a smile. She completed the forms and led him out front to a waiting Fiat Strada sedan. Fine. It would be ample for the trip. He thanked the girl and motored around the Piazza until he found an open spot. As he pulled in, an elderly Italian man, slovenly dressed in patched trousers and bulky sweater against the early spring chill, approached the car. He rubbed his thumb and index finger together, then pointed to the car.

"*Signore* . . . to watch."

Kolnikov cursed under his breath. He had forgotten about the Neopolitan system of "protection" for parked cars. Each block on every street is divided into territories watched over by a "guard," who pays part of his take back to the mob for his "franchise." You pay, or your car is gone in an hour. On the other hand, it could also work for you; at least you knew your car *wouldn't* be stolen. There is no *un*organized crime in Naples.

Kolnikov gave the "guardian" five thousand lire *"per tre giorni"*—three days. The man thanked him graciously with a tip of his cap—all guardians wear them as symbol

168

of their sacred office—and departed for another car which was pulling into a space nearby and would urgently need his invaluable services.

Gruber and Lowell were doing their best to look like innocent tourists when Kolnikov returned. He had several newspapers tucked under his arm and a book in his hand; he handed that to Lowell first.

"Here's your book. *The Thorn Birds.* Sort of looks like you." Lowell grinned. "They also had *Assault on a Queen,* but that might be pushing Lady Luck a bit far. Any action?"

Both men shook their heads. Kolnikov passed out the papers, keeping the *Rome Daily American* for himself.

"I found out why all the fuss," he said, pointing to the lead story.

"We already know," rejoined Gruber. Kolnikov looked startled. "We asked the waiter why all the excitement. He says the US is threatening war with Russia over this incident in Turkey. That the Soviets have nearly forty divisions on Turkey's northeastern border, with another several dozen Russians, Bulgarian, and Roumanian divisions on the border just west of Istanbul."

Kolnikov frowned. "That's more than it says in here."

"It always is. But the waiter says he's got the straight poop; claims his brother's sister's living with one of the Communications officers up at COMSOUTH Headquarters."

"Then, we believe *him.*"

169

THIRTY-ONE

VICTOR HAD just put a pillow over his head to shut out the sunlight when Lowell burst into the room.

"Victor! Max! Wake up! They've done it!"

Kolnikov ducked back out from under the pillow.

"Are you sure?"

"Sure I'm sure! It was just like you told me: a Lieutenant JG and three Petty Officers, each with a forty-five—and there was a clip in each one—and six Marines with Thompsons. They got into two jeeps and drove off up the Piazza with two jeeploads of Italian cops —one in front and one aft. They also had machineguns."

Victor looked at his watch. It was just eight-twenty.

"Did you say *three* Petty Officers with him?"

"Yes. And six Marines."

Max was sitting up in bed by now. Victor smiled first at Lowell, then at Gruber.

"*Three* assistants, a total of four. How many bags were they carrying. Did you notice, Jon?"

"Two apiece. Big ones."

"That means a *big* one. They've probably drawn three months' worth."

Gruber leaned over toward Kolnikov. "But

we won't be able to carry that much off, Victor."

"Yes, Max. But that makes it even better. We'll only have to take the big bills—the cream off the top—to make a full haul; we won't even have to bother about the foreign stuff. Good!"

And with a look of self-satisfaction, he lay back on the bed and readied his pillow. Lowell was still standing in the middle of the room.

"Take your clothes off and lie down for awhile, Jon—might as well relax while you can."

"But what about the money . . ."

Victor turned back. "It'll take them at least two hours to get to the base, make the draw, get back to the ship, and stow it. They won't be done until noon. So we'll hit 'em after lunch."

Lowell undressed, climbed into bed, and lay there wondering how one slept with one's eyes jammed wide open.

THIRTY-TWO

"I'LL HAVE to see your papers, Commander."

The youthful-looking Ensign in charge of the boats was polite but firm. No one not on official business was to be allowed out to the ship. Orders from the Admiral. Kolnikov produced his. The officer read them and handed them back.

"Are these men part of your official party?"

"Yes, they are."

"Then you can all board right now, sir, the boat will leave in about five minutes."

Just then, a well-dressed woman in her late thirties who had been speaking with the Boat Officer when Kolnikov's group approached accosted Victor. She was the type of wife who wore her rank more importantly than her husband.

"Commander . . . this officer won't let me go aboard . . . says there's something about orders. My husband is Captain Barnett, in charge of the Air Group. Can't you help me?" Her words were very much in the way of a command, having established her husband's seniority to Victor. Kolnikov turned and shook his head.

"Orders are orders, ma'am. But if it's an emergency, I suggest you see the Port Officer over there." He indicated a low shack of a building almost hidden between walls of crates.

"But I need to go out right away. Could you hold the boat?"

"You'll have to ask the Boat Officer here. I'm not attached to the ship, and . . ."

"Say, don't I know you?"

Victor's heart ran down and hid in his guts. "Perhaps," he mumbled, glancing away at the other two. Gruber jabbed Lowell and pointed to the five large black bags that lay beside them on the dock; they started picking them up and transferring them down into the boat.

"Wasn't it *Victor* . . . er, something?"

"I'm Vasyli Kolchov . . . Supply Corps, Finance Office, Washington."

The woman cocked her head.

"No, I guess not. The name was close, though. But I think he was in Intelligence."

Victor could feel his hair turning grayer. The Boat Officer stepped over just then.

"The boat's leaving now, Commander."

Kolnikov grabbed the opportunity to disengage and clambered down into the small officers' motorboat. The woman was still arguing with the Ensign when they pulled away from the dock. Except for the coxswain and one boatswain, they were alone. Despite the chill breeze in the open sternsheets, Victor was sweating profusely. He produced a handkerchief, took off his cap, and started mopping his brow.

"That was a close one. And I hope it's the last."

Gruber and Lowell just stared as if in shock.

"You know, Max, I think we should have taken your suggestion and had a drink or two before we started out."

"I did. And it didn't do any good." He held up his hand, it was shaking.

"And there won't be any out there," Kolnikov offered. "Fortunately, we should be on and off in less than a half hour."

"That quick?"

"Yeah. That quick."

All three lapsed into contemplative silence as they watched the *Forrestal*. Never exactly small—even all the way out there—it got bigger, and bigger and bigger.

Until it looked almost as big as the island they'd left the day before.

THIRTY-THREE

LIEUTENANT COMMANDER Vasyli M. Kolchov, SC, USN, saluted the Officer-of-the-Deck and showed him his orders.

"I'd like to see the Disbursing Officer immediately."

"Yes, sir. Right away. Please wait over here with your men." The immaculately turned out and spitshined Lieutenant gestured to one of the sailors on the small Quarterdeck. "Bo'sun. Pass the word for Lieutenant JG Black to report to the Quarterdeck."

The sailor saluted, moved smartly over to a bank of dials and buttons, and picked up a small black hand microphone labeled "1 M.C."

"Lieutenant JG Black. Please report to the Quarterdeck." Multiplied by a hundred loudspeakers in and about the ship, the command cut clearly through the cacophony of the busy supercarrier and rolled echoing away across the water.

A few minutes later, a slender, athletic-looking officer in working blue uniform climbed up the ladder from the deck below and stepped over the hatch combing onto the Quarterdeck. The OD, in conversation with two other officers, pointed him over to Kolnikov's group.

"Lieutenant JG Black, sir," he announced, saluting. "What can I do for you?"

Kolnikov saluted and introduced himself. Then he showed the junior man his orders. Black visibly wilted.

"An audit? Oh shoot!" He looked pleadingly at Kolnikov. "We just drew from COM-SOUTH Bank this morning . . . it'll take a *day* to count all that. And we're on standby to pull out the minute we've got everything aboard." He looked around, as if seeking support from someone . . . anyone . . . the ship's Supply Officer maybe? "Can't this be delayed, Commander?"

Kolnikov demurred. "I'm afraid not. But maybe we can speed things up. Have you unbundled everything yet?"

"Not quite everything, sir. We only got back just before lunch."

"Then let's go to the Disbursing Office. Depending on what we find, we may be able to get this done in a couple of hours."

As the young man conveyed Kolnikov and the other two down through the interconnecting maze of passageways, corridors, and hatches which make up the lower spaces of a carrier, Kolnikov studied him. He was Mister Clean. Obviously didn't swear, most likely didn't smoke or drink either. His neat-cropped sandy hair atop clear, brown eyes on a friendly open face—the kind that tells everything it knows—his earnest expression and purposeful walk all added up to the Supply image. Not the swashbuckler in any way. In civilian life he'd be perfect as a banker. He was exactly what Kolnikov expected. His high morals and sense of duty would certainly rebel at what was about to happen to him. He'd be caught in a terrible conflict between the commandments of his Lord and his love for his family. Still, Kolnikov counted on those very characteristics working for him. Because he was so straight, he would be totally unprepared. Without a crooked bone in his body, and caught by surprise, he'd panic—and the deed would be done before he could get his head thinking again.

Kolnikov breathed a little easier. He knew his psychology. And Roger Black was the best possible type he could have drawn.

After what seemed like an endless trip through a labyrinthine nether world, they arrived at a door marked "Disbursing Officer." It was unlocked. Two enlisted men who had been relaxing over a game of acey-deucy snapped to attention as they entered. Black turned to Kolnikov.

"These are my two assistant paymasters, Commander. I know it isn't SOP, but maybe if they could help your people with the count, it might go faster. So if you wish . . ."

Kolnikov cut him short.

"That won't be necessary. Not for the moment."

Looking a bit crestfallen, Black reluctantly dismissed the two men, locking the door to the office after they departed. He turned to Kolnikov.

"What first, Commander?"

"Is all your cash stowed?"

"Certainly, sir." Black gave Victor a look of mixed puzzlement and hurt that it should be suspected otherwise, though some Disbursing Officers have been notoriously sloppy about procedures—Victor had met some of the unluckier ones in Portsmouth.

"Then open up, and we can get started."

"What about my ledgers, sir?"

"Yes. Get those and then open up."

Black hefted the bulky looseleaf ledgers over to the long counting table next to what appeared to be his desk, then made his silent incantations over the dual combination locks of the safe. Kolnikov looked at his two conspirators. Lowell looked as if he were going to fall down. Victor motioned him to sit. Gruber he silently signaled to block the doorway. As he had briefed Max earlier, if Black did put up a fight, if it came to that, they would simply put him out of action, take the money, and run. But only as a last resort. It would be very risky. Much of the success of Victor's plans rested on their having all the time they needed to get to Rome and away before the tocsin sounded.

As the door of the safe swung open, Gruber failed to suppress a low whistle. Kolnikov shot him a black look. "Christ! I've never seen so much in a safe this size," he exclaimed, covering his *faux pas*. Black turned and beamed.

"Neither have I. But they told us to draw for three months. There's more than seven and a half million in there, not counting foreign currency."

Kolnikov, Gruber, and Lowell stood mesmerized for several seconds. There was not an inch of space not taken up by bundles of banknotes. Black pointed at the cornucopia.

"Actually, Commander, there was so much we had to put our coins in one of the Medical Officer's narcotics safes." He was obviously proud of the size of the treasure entrusted to him.

"Well, then," drawled Kolnikov, "we'll speed things up by just counting the paper."

The Disbursing Officer sighed in relief and, turning back toward the safe, began collecting its bulging contents. Victor beamed at the other two. Even Lowell managed a smile, relieved that things had gone smoothly so far. Black laid an armful up on the table. Victor motioned to Gruber and Lowell.

"Bear a hand with Mister Black here. Get them all stacked up on the other end of the table so there'll be room for us to count it as it goes back in."

It still took nearly ten minutes for the three, aided by Kolnikov, to pile and arrange the packets into equal stacks. When they were done, the Naval-neat palisade of currency stretched to both sides, and more than halfway down the table. Everything was stacked by type and denomination—one hundreds, fifties, twenties, tens, etc.—with similar piles of foreign monies, especially Greek drachma notes and the colorful, slightly exotic Turkish dinars. As he carefully topped off the last stack, Black put his head over on one side.

"I hope you people plan t'set a piece. There's enough to keep us busy all the way to Turkey."

"I don't think we'll try to count it here— not all this." Kolnikov tried to sound as matter-of-fact as possible. Black looked up startled. Gruber moved unobtrusively toward the door.

"Not count it here? Then where?"

"If, as you say, you're leaving momentarily, we may have to conduct this count on the beach, then fly it back out."

Black was dumbfounded. He looked around the office as if searching for some Navy manual that authorized a procedure such as this.

"But . . . but, Commander, we just *drew* all this, this morning. We . . . we need it." He stopped, struggling to regain his mental footing. Finally, a thought struck him. He picked up the telephone on the desk. "I'll have to clear this with the Supply Officer." He started to dial. Kolnikov stepped over and pressed his finger down on the cradle.

"That won't be necessary, Lieutenant." Black was now completely confused. He gaped at Kolnikov.

"But Commander, this is completely irregular, I . . ."

"Put the phone down, Mister!" Kolnikov's command hit Black squarely amidships. He slowly replaced the receiver. Kolnikov regarded him coldly.

"Now, sit down!" Kolnikov produced the photographs. He arranged them out on the desk. Marilu Black and her two children smiled happily up at their surprised father. So did Victor Kolnikov. Black picked up one, then another at random, almost idly, turning each over on its back as if expecting to find the real people there.

"I don't understand, Commander . . . when . . ."

"They were taken Saturday."

"But, I don't understand." Something told Roger Black that something terrible was about to happen. His voice was a plaintive whine.

"Then let me explain. Those are your wife and children?" Black nodded eagerly, as if trying to affirm their existence. "And if you ever want to see them again—alive—you are *not* going to phone the Supply Officer. You are going to help us pack this money into these bags here. Then you are going to accompany us ashore and . . ." Kolnikov paused. "You will do exactly what you are told thereafter." He paused again. "Or, as I said, Mr. Black, you will never see your wife or children alive."

Black looked up at Kolnikov. Then at Gruber and Lowell. He was in shock, his mind fighting the comprehension of Victor's words.

"But what do you want? Why . . ."

"We want the money, Black. And you're going to help us. IS THAT CLEAR?" Kolnikov's face was a devil's mask. Every psychological ploy Victor had ever learned in Intelligence about dominating men was now coming into play against his unfortunate victim, who still sat transfixed, a photograph in each hand.

"DID YOU HEAR ME, BLACK?" The young man recoiled.

"But I can't do . . ."

"You can and you will, Black. If you love

your family. We're not bluffing and we're not kidding."

"But, Marilu and the children . . ."

"They're safe—for the moment. Our people have them, and they haven't been harmed. Nor will they be—*if* you cooperate."

"What do you want me to do?"

"Exactly as I told you. We're going to pack up this money and go ashore. From there, we'll tell you what to do next. If you do your part, you and they will be all right. If not—well, I've told you that part."

Black pitched forward and hid his face in his hands. "Oh, Lord! Lord!" He started to cry. Kolnikov let him. He turned to Gruber and Lowell.

"Start packing those bags. Pack 'em tight, and start with the biggest bills and work down from there."

Black tried to stand up. His legs wouldn't let him.

"Hey! You can't . . ."

"We can and we are, Black. Now, are you going to cooperate or not?" Black looked up at Kolnikov through tear-reddened eyes.

"Do I have any choice?"

"None at all." Kolnikov's voice was as flat as a becalmed sea. "If you don't cooperate with us, we'll kill you—here and now. And then your family. And we'll still have the money. And if you try anything foolish, and we get caught . . . our people have orders to execute them if they don't get the right message from us before twelve-hundred on Tuesday."

Black looked ghastly. He had stopped

crying and started to sweat. Kolnikov patted him on the shoulder.

"You just sit there, Roger, and calm yourself down while we finish here. We won't need your help yet." Kolnikov surveyed the shaken officer. "But do get yourself calmed down—and *fast*—because we're leaving *with* you, and you had better look fit and chipper. Okay?"

Black nodded. It was then that Victor noticed the .45 Colt automatic still in its holster where Black had hung it up that morning. He leaned over and took it out. Retrieving one of the two clips from the holster belt, he slid it into the handle, cocked the bolt, set the safety, and slipped it in his belt, underneath the front of his jacket. "Black?" The young man looked up. "Just in case you get any heroic ideas on the way out, I've got this." He patted the coat. Then he turned to Gruber and Lowell.

"How much longer?"

"About ten minutes, Victor," replied Gruber stuffing as fast as he could. "Christ! Seven million dollars is a lot of fuckin' paper."

"Well, only take what will fit. We'll leave the small stuff for the next guy."

The thought of leaving so much money as virtual crumbs nearly overwhelmed Gruber. "Jesus Fucking Christ! I don't fucking *believe* it!"

"You will when you start spending it," chuckled Kolnikov. He looked at his watch. It was just fourteen-twenty-five. They had been aboard less than forty minutes. "What time's

183

the next officers' boat?" Black started from his stupor. "Fifteen-hundred, Commander." Kolnikov noted the last, and approved; Black was fully under his domination—even addressing him as "Commander." Good! That meant he'd play his part.

"Okay then. Let's finish up our packing." Victor looked around the office. "Where are your bags, Roger?" Black pointed to several shoved under a desk.

"Take two of them and start filling up." Black shuffled over and dug out the bags, moving slowly, automatically.

Kolnikov moved over to where Gruber and Lowell were feverishly stuffing the massive hoard into the large satchels as quickly as they could snatch yet another bundle and find a niche for it. He called to Black, who was still fumbling under the desk.

"C'mon, Black. On the double." Black jumped back slightly, then hurried to the table with his bags. "Okay. Fill 'em up—now, Mister!" Black started moving as fast as the other two.

THIRTY-FOUR

BLACK AND LOWELL had just forced the tops of the last two bags shut and Gruber had begun realigning them on the tables when the steady background hum of the ship was suddenly overwhelmed by a raucous bonging which reverberated from the 1 M.C. loudspeaker—followed instantly by the ear-splitting trill of a boatswain's pipe.

"SET THE EMERGENCY SEA DETAIL! SET THE EMERGENCY SEA DETAIL! PREPARE TO GET UNDERWAY! ALL HANDS MAN YOUR BATTLE STATIONS FOR LEAVING PORT! THIS IS NO DRILL! REPEAT! THIS IS NO DRILL!"

Suddenly, the passageway outside the Disbursing Office erupted into a purposeful pandemonium of running men and shouted orders. The boatswain pipe shrilled again.

"SET MODIFIED CONDITION ZEBRA! REPEAT! SET MODIFIED CONDITION ZEBRA."

Inside the Disbursing Office there was modified pandemonium on the faces of all four men there. Kolnikov, the most experienced sailor, was the first to recover.

"Quick—get those bags! You, too, Black! And get ready to follow me!" He turned the key in the lock and looked out cautiously, then turned back.

"Mister Black. Come up here in front of

me." Black lifted his two bags and joined Kolnikov by the partially opened door.

"Remember what I said, Roger?" A nod. "Then, you go first . . . right in front of me . . . take us *directly* to the Quarterdeck." He turned to the other two. Gruber passed Kolnikov one of the last three bags on the table, then took the other two himself. They were all in line.

"Okay, Roger. Now!" Kolnikov prodded him; he took off to the right, headed straight for the nearest starboard ladder.

Snaking and colliding their way through the rushing humanity, they emerged on the Hangar Deck, just aft of the Quarterdeck. A dozen more strides and they were there.

The OD was the center of a hailstorm of running men, ringing phones and shouted orders. Leaving the rest, Kolnikov made his way over to the harried Lieutenant.

"We have to get ashore. Is there a boat available?"

The Lieutenant spun angrily, then straightened as he spotted seniority. "Not from here, Commander!" he called over the din of urgent, competing voices. He emphasized the finality of his answer by directing Kolnikov's attention to the boat davits. The officers' motorboat was being swung in, still dripping seawater. Four decks below, the Captain's Gig had just broken water; men were leaning over the inboard gunwales, steadying her swing with long boathooks. Seeing Kolnikov's expression—and perhaps wanting this additional problem out of his domain— he pointed aft.

"Try the after bow. They may still have one, though I doubt it."

Kolnikov wheeled and charged past the others, headed for the larger, busier enlisted-and-supplies loading area at the diametrically opposite end of the huge ship.

Things were no better there. Kolnikov could tell the moment he arrived. One last open launch was circling in toward the waiting cables, spurred on by the bellowing baritone of a First-Class Boatswain's Mate on the Boat Deck who seemed amply blessed with a talent for stringing together whole sentences without the use of a single unprofane word. The Junior Officer of the Deck was, if possible, even more harried than the OD when Kolnikov reached the rail.

"I need a boat, Mister."

"There's nothing, sir. Absolutely nothing. We're even leaving two launches on the beach. No time to wait for them to come out." He looked down at the water. "In fact, we're underway right now." Kolnikov looked down and cursed. There was no mistaking the steady, though slow, drift of flotsom as it bobbed and cavorted aftward.

One last hope, a local barge manned by Neopolitans, its skipper gesticulating and cursing over the sudden *coitus interruptus* of his own unloading of supplies, had already drifted out of earshot.

The JOD joined Kolnikov at the rail to observe the lifting of the last boat. He was genuinely solicitous of Kolnikov's plight.

"You can try the flight deck, sir. You might get a helo. Otherwise, you'll have to wait for a shuttle flight." The Ensign frowned as his gaze met Kolnikov's face. For a moment, he debated calling sickbay.

THIRTY-FIVE

KOLNIKOV TURNED the key in the Disbursing Office door, and heaved his bag up onto the table with the rest. Then he stopped to catch his breath. After the frantic dash, first to the Quarterdeck, then the After Brow, the trek back through Modified Condition ZEBRA had been a seemingly endless succession of hatches—each one of which had to be un-dogged, opened, then shut and redogged—with the bags not only getting heavier but seeming more conspicuous every step of the way.

Gruber, ever impatient, was the first to find his voice. "Why didn't we go straight to the Flight Deck, Victor?"

"With these?" He jerked his thumb at the array on the table. "First, we couldn't have gotten everything and all of us on a single helicopter. We'd probably get stuck up there, and with all this gear somebody'd be bound to ask questions." He walked over to the desk and slumped into the chair. For a moment he struggled with the rising panic in his throat before speaking again.

"No. We'll have to try and get on the first shuttle flight to the beach."

"How soon will that be?"

"I can't say. But we can figure on at least an hour before she's gained enough sea room for a normal launch and recovery."

"How do you know she'll even do it?" interjected Lowell, who had found a seat opposite Victor and was now fanning himself with his hat.

"She'll have to. She pulled out so fast, she *had* to strand half an army on the beach, and they'll all head for the airbase and wait for the birds to come in and pick them up. It happens all the time with carriers—and at least on a carrier you get picked up; in the blackshoe Navy you have to make your way to your ship's next port or find yourself some Jesus Shoes."

Lowell managed a nervous smile. It made Kolnikov realize how much like Black he was. Where was Black? Victor looked around and spied him slumped in a chair behind Gruber, who was still standing.

"Roger." Black leaned foward and stared apprehensively at Kolnikov. "I want you to find out when the first shuttle plane departs." Black pointed toward the desk at which Victor was seated.

"Why not just call AIR-OPS?"

Why not indeed? Victor should have thought of that himself. He lit a cigarette to steady himself; this was no time to let oneself get unraveled. Then he dialed the number listed on the card taped to the bulkhead above the desk. Yes, there would be a flight in about forty minutes. Four men and nine bags? Is it priority? Very well, then. But would the Commander be kind enough to come up to the Line Shack with his orders to verify his priority?

"Thank you," said Kolnikov and hung up. "Okay, Roger—you're on!"

THIRTY-SIX

KOLNIKOV AND Black swung out of the thwart-ships passage where the Disbursing Office was located and started down one of the two long corridors which run the length of the ship—port and starboard—just under the busy hangar deck. Ten minutes earlier the ship had secured from General Quarters, and the going was infinitely easier; one could see the entire length of the corridor now, and it looked as if it should bend over the horizon. The Captain was apparently putting as much ocean between his ship and the land as possible, because they could both feel the rumble of her four thirty-ton screws biting in the water even this far forward.

Just before they reached the escalator to the Flight Deck, Kolnikov noticed the entrance to the Officers' Wardroom. He stopped Black just before the later stepped onto the four-deck-high moving stair.

"We've got a few minutes, Roger. Let's stop for a cup of coffee. I need one, and you *look* like you need one, if not something stronger."

As Victor reached the open doorway, he suddenly bolted backward so violently he collided with Black and nearly sent the smaller man sprawling. Spinning sideways, Kolnikov grabbed him.

"Roger," he hissed urgently, "I forget . . . where's the other door to this place?"

"Right this way, Commander." The

startled Black led the big man to a door a few yards further down the corridor. By now, he was surprised by nothing this strange man did; besides, he was more concerned with getting this whole thing over and having Marilu and the children safe.

The door led into the Senior Officers' Dining Room. Kolnikov went in first, Black behind him. The room was dark and separated from the brightly lighted Wardroom by a heavy double curtain.

Kolnikov led Black to a corner from which they could observe the adjoining area without being seen themselves. As they stood together in the darkness, Kolnikov parted the curtain slightly, peered out, then motioned Black to do likewise.

"That Commander sitting on the couch drinking coffee with the two JGs . . . who is he?" Kolnikov whispered.

Black took a second look and stepped back.

"He's new. Less than a month. His name's Hartranft."

"Hartranft?"

"Yessir. He's the new Chief of the W Division."

"The WHAT?" Kolnikov almost forgot himself. He moved them both further back into the darkened dining room.

"Are you sure, Roger?"

"Absolutely, Commander. I have his pay record." Black peered at Kolnikov through the partial gloom. "Are you all right, sir?"

Kolnikov couldn't be sure. Not if Arnold Gelman was in charge of the Nuclear Weapons Division of the U.S.S. *Forrestal!*

THIRTY-SEVEN

KOLNIKOV LED a very confused Black back out
the door into the corridor. Once outside, he
turned and leaned head first against the bulkhead. He was trying desperately to make the
maelstrom in his brain slow down. It
wouldn't.

Black repeated his earlier question. "Are
you all right, sir?" Kolnikov straightened up
and blinked his eyes several times hard. He
placed his hand against the bulkhead as if to
keep from reeling.

"I don't know, Roger." He looked around.
"Tell me . . . is the Personnel Office still in the
same place it used to be?"

Black gave him an uncomprehending look.
How could he know where it used to be?

"Wherever it is, Roger . . . take me there—
fast!"

Black led them to a door about fifty yards
aft marked "Admin Office." In the rear was a
section marked "Personnel Office," partially
divided from the front, with several desks
and file cabinets. A Third-Class Personnel-
man in working dungarees was busy
replacing file folders. He braced as Kolnikov
and Black approached him. Kolnikov stepped
straight over to the cabinets.

"At ease, sailor. Let me see the personnel
files for the W Division."

"But Sir, I'm not permitted to . . ."

"I'll take the responsibility sailor. Now, where are they?" The sailor indicated the second drawer from the top of the far left-hand cabinet, then turned back to his own work.

Kolnikov found what he was looking for immediately. Good old Navy neatness and organization! The dark buff manila folder marked "Hartranft, Harold L., CDR 627723-1105W" was thick, as a Commander's should be. Victor sorted through the papers slowly, carefully, almost unbelievingly. The photographs, front and profile, they were Gelman, all right—a decade older than Victor's last mental picture of him but unmistakable. The rest was what impressed him. O.C.S. Certificate, copies of duty and travel orders and DD-214s, Navy schools—including Nuclear Weapons School ten years ago—a complete service record including every level of background check and security clearance. And every bit of it phony. Or was it? Could he be wrong? Could it be just a chance phenomenal resemblance? The mass of documentation in his hand was undermining his confidence.

What he saw next restored it.

Two more folders reposed in the drawer behind Hartranft's.

"Dyer, John W., LCDR, 973665-1100W."

"Fisher, Charles E., WO-4, 162-28-3054W."

Each a complete service record, fully documented for the jobs they held. Everything was in perfect order. Except for the photos. Front and profile. Horn and Stoddard!

THIRTY-EIGHT

KOLNIKOV USHERED Black through the Disbursing Office door and locked it behind them. As he turned to speak, the 1 M.C. blared out: "LIEUTENANT COMMANDER KOLCHOV AND PARTY, PLEASE REPORT TO THE FLIGHT DECK. LIEUTENANT COMMANDER KOLCHOV AND PARTY, PLEASE REPORT TO THE FLIGHT DECK." Gruber jumped up from his seat; Lowell rose as well.

"Eureka, Victor—that's us. Y'did it, Old Buddy. Let's go." Gruber grabbed a bag and handed it to Victor, then swung two over toward Black. Kolnikov set his down and stopped the other two in midswing.

"Not just yet, Max."

"But that's our flight, Victor. We gotta get up there on the double!" Gruber kept trying to hand the bags to Black; Kolnikov kept pushing them back. The strain of the last two hours broke through in Gruber's voice as it swept up in pitch and intensity. "C'mon, Victor. Pick up your bag and let's GET GOING!" Kolnikov stepped squarely in front of Gruber and glared at him.

"I said, *hold it*, Max . . . now put those bags up. And *listen* to me!" Victor grabbed the bags from Gruber and slammed them down hard on the table. Gruber raised his hands in supplication; his mouth worked, but nothing much would come out.

Lowell had already replaced his heavy load on the table. Gruber raised his head and looked around wide-eyed, like an animal in pain seeking the source of the wounding arrow.

"Sit down, Max," ordered Kolnikov. Gruber stared at him dumbly. "I said sit down—now." Victor's voice was calm now and it had a quieting effect on Gruber, who hopped up on the table, looked at Lowell, and shrugged resignedly.

Kolnikov took the time to fix each man with his eyes before dropping the bombshell.

"Gentlemen," he intoned slowly, "the situation has changed . . . radically . . . something's come up. I don't know why or how but . . ."

"But what?" Gruber was back on the attack. "Isn't that our flight? Aren't we clear to go?"

"No, Max. We aren't. Gelman, Horn, and Stoddard are on this ship. Gelman is in charge of the W Division, and Horn and Stoddard are his two assistants."

Lowell looked up at Kolnikov. "What's the W Division?"

"All the ship's nuclear weapons," interjected Gruber, recovering from his second shook in as many minutes. Then he looked incredulous. "Are you sure, Victor? I mean . . . how did you find out? I don't . . ."

Kolnikov had been holding three sheets of paper in his left hand. Now he handed them to Gruber, who unrolled them. They were photocopies of the first page of Gelman's, Horn's, and Stoddard's service records including each one's photo: the photos of men identified as Hartranft, Dyer, and Fisher.

Gruber, with Lowell peering over his shoulder, studied them in stunned silence. It was several minutes before Gruber responded.

"I don't believe it, Victor."

"I didn't think you would. That's why I made those copies. I'm not sure I believe it myself."

"But why . . . why here?"

"I don't know. But there are three complete, completely phony service records up there in Personnel. Complete histories, duty stations, DD-124s, background checks, and clearances, Nuclear Weapons School for all three—all of it set up to qualify them for where they are right now." Victor paused to let this sink in.

"Do you realize, Max, what all that took? All the work? All the coverups? The time? The people? Do you realize what all this adds up to?"

"I'm beginning to, Victor."

"What's more, these three are just the tip of the iceberg. It'd take a dozen—two dozen— people, all in the right place, to pull this off." Gruber assented. "And remember what Simon said? That he suspected people higher up—even in other agencies?"

"Yes."

"They had to have that too. Otherwise something in those files would've bounced a mile high. Max, those FBI background checks couldn't be phonied safely; they have to've had somebody in the Bureau. Christ, Max! This isn't a uniform and a couple of sets of phony orders and an ID card or two. This had to be done by a whole interconnecting hierarchy of agents, each one planted in exactly the right place. And it would have taken *years!*"

"How *many* years, Victor?"

"Would you believe . . . *nine?*"

Gruber closed his eyes. "Oh, my God!"

Kolnikov's next words were drowned out by the 1 M.C. "LIEUTENANT COMMANDER KOLCHOV AND PARTY. PLEASE REPORT TO THE FLIGHT DECK, ON THE DOUBLE. LIEUTENANT COMMANDER KOLCHOV AND PARTY, PLEASE REPORT TO THE FLIGHT DECK ON THE DOUBLE."

Kolnikov motioned to Black. "Phone them. Tell them we've been delayed. That we'll have to take a later flight." Black bent over the desk and started dialing. Gruber hopped off the tabletop.

"But what about us? If we wait for a later flight, they might spot us and maybe blow the whole thing." His face suddenly lit up. "Unless, of course, you're waiting for a night flight, when they're less likely to recognize us?"

"No, Max. We're not going . . . or, at least I'm not."

"Not going? But, if they haven't spotted us, we can still make it—and still do like you said. We even know where they are."

"That's not the point. This puts us into a whole new ballgame." Victor tapped the papers. "Don't you see? This is the big hit Simon talked about, the one they've taken years to put together." Kolnikov whirled around, as if keeping up with his head; he slammed his fist into his other hand as each piece fell into place.

"But can you be sure this is the Big Show and not just a diversion?"

"It could be a diversion, Max. But I doubt it. It took too much. They had to stick out too many necks to set this up. No, Max. Something is going down. Right here on the *Forrestal*. Something *very* big. And soon. And my guess is this business with Turkey is part of it. And we've got to find out what and stop it."

Gruber wasn't being fended off. "We could still do it." He walked around Victor as he talked. "Look . . . we can split. And then inform Roschestvensky. We could do it by radiogram from the plane once we're safely on our way. You said yourself you couldn't give a damn about vindication . . . or Naval Intelligence . . . or the Navy, for that matter."

"But I still do, Max." Lowell had joined the group. He instinctively stood next to Kolnikov.

"Then you stay if you want to. But I say you and I should go, Victor."

Kolnikov shook his head. "Not me, Max. Not now. I still feel the same way. But there's something here that's too big to just walk out on. I'm staying. If you want to go—go." Kolnikov set his jaw, a signal both men knew too well to continue against. Gruber collapsed into a chair.

"Okay, Victor. We'll play it your way." He looked at the assemblage on the table. "But . . . all that . . . fucking . . . *money!*"

THIRTY-NINE

VICTOR WAS suddenly aware of Roger Black. He hadn't moved since phoning FLIGHT OPS. His open, country face was that of a child watching a movie completely beyond his comprehension yet strangely entrancing—or a mental patient who has found reality too kaleidoscopic for endurance. Kolnikov's mind shifted into another equally high gear.

How could he—now—shift this basically simple, straight-forward kid's gears without stripping them entirely? Victor walked over to Black and placed a fatherly hand on his shoulder.

"Open the safe, son."

"What? Er . . . sir?"

"I said, open the safe."

Black moved like a somnambulist. He hunkered down and began spinning the dials; he made no attempt to shield them from view with his body, gave no thought to protecting the secret of the combinations only he alone knew. Then he swung the heavy doors open. Kolnikov started opening the first bag.

"Okay, men. Let's put it back." He turned to Gruber. "*All* of it. You, too, Roger. Show us where it goes."

Shaken awake by this last act in the afternoon's melodrama, Black started babbling. "But . . . but Commander . . . the money . . . isn't that what you wanted!"

"Not now, son. Start packing it in there."
Kolnikov dumped a pile of bundled currency
into Black's arms. A few packets tumbled
onto the floor. Kolnikov bent down, retrieved
them, and placed them on top of the pile.
Suddenly Black dropped the whole pile. He
blanched.

"What about Marilu and my children?"

Victor put both hands on Black's shoulders
and spoke squarely into his face. "They're
safe and sound. They always were. There's
nobody back in Norfolk. There's just us here.
The photos were a pure bluff. Believe me,
son, they're safe. I took those pictures last
Saturday myself—alone." Kolnikov eased
him over to the desk. "Look, Roger. That one
with me and the little ones? Marilu took it. If
anybody else'd been there with me, we'd both
be in it, wouldn't we?"

Black slumped into the chair and started
sobbing uncontrollably. Kolnikov turned
back to the two at the safe.

"Okay. Let's all bear a hand and get it in
there and lock up. He can straighten it up
later."

A few minutes later, Kolnikov swung the
safe doors shut with a reassuring clunk.
Black had recovered from his hysteria but
still looked shellshocked.

"All right, son. There it is all safe and
sound. The money. Your wife and kids."
Victor reached under his coat. "And here's
your pistol. The masquerade's over."

Black took the automatic, disarmed it, and
slipped it back into its holster. Then he
grimaced up at Kolnikov.

"But why? Why all this?"

"It would take too long to explain, and I'm not certain you'd understand if we did. But right now we need your help. Will you help us?"

"I . . ." Black looked around again for the appropriate Navy Manual. "I don't know . . . I . . ."

Now Kolnikov played his cards. He pulled a chair up next to Black's, sat down, and clapped his giant's paw over the young man's shoulder again.

"Look, son. An hour ago, we were ready to leave with you and six million dollars. Right? And we would have made it. Right? And it would've probably gotten you busted right out of the Navy, if not into Fort Leavenworth. Right? And you thought your wife and children would be hurt. Right? But now the money's all back in the safe—every penny. Right? And Marilu and the children . . ."

Black nodded on cue at each point in Victor's exposition. Watching the performance, Gruber sidled over to Lowell and whispered to him:

"Jon, d'you remember that old flick, *Of Mice and Men* . . . the part at the end where Burgess Meridith feeds Lon Chaney—who played Lenny—all that bullshit just before he blew his brains out . . . remember?" Lowell managed a guilty smile. "The only thing here, Jon, is . . ." Gruber struggled to suppress the laughter threatening to overwhelm him. "With Victor, it looks . . . THE OTHER WAY AROUND!"

FORTY

ROGER BLACK unlocked the door to his stateroom and showed them in.

"Here it is, Commander. It's the best I can do for now."

The stateroom was dark, save for the fluorescent light that shone down on the small metal utility desk sandwiched between two large lockers. The overhead was the usual jumble of water pipes, air ducts, electrical conduits, and exposed steel beams—all painted a dull Navy standard gray. Two more lockers, another desk, and a set of double bunks against the far bulkhead completed the picture. Two spare metal and plastic chairs were placed with military neatness against each desk. Though more spacious than some other staterooms, First Class on the Q.E. II it wasn't. Down here, on the second deck below the Hangar Deck, the rumble of the screws was even more noticeable, and every few minutes the background hums of the ship were punctuated by a jolt that seemed to rattle every rivet. Lowell was getting more apprehensive over this strange phenomenon which seemed to threaten to tear the ship apart.

"What's that noise?" he asked Black, looking around as if expecting to see a leak burst forth any second.

"That's the catapults. We must be at Flight

Quarters," he answered, then turned to Kolnikov.

"There's no one staying here but me, and I can bunk across the passage with the Wardroom Officer, Lieutenant JG Schermerhorn. Incidentally, he's the one I'll get to arrange for you people to be fed down here so you won't have to use the Wardroom or Mess Decks." He looked at Gruber's and Lowell's uniforms. "I'll explain that you're all officers on a hush-hush mission. He's a great guy, and we can trust him to keep his mouth shut. How long will you be here, Commander?"

"I don't know, Roger. Not long, I hope. It should only be a day or two."

"All right, then, gentlemen. I'll get some more clean towels . . . my shaving gear is over the sink and the head is down the passageway aft. Now I have to get back and explain my absence during General Quarters. Anything else?"

"Yes, Roger, just one more thing." Victor had been carrying a sheaf of Navy message blanks which he had picked up in the Disbursing Office. He pulled the chair back from the lighted desk, sat down, peeled off a triplicated blank, and wrote.

When he was finished, he passed it to Gruber and Lowell:

PRIORITY
TO: CAPT SIMON ROSCHESTVENSKY
    ONI-COUNTER INTEL
    WASHINGTON

GELMAN. HORN. STODDARD. BINGO.

As Lowell handed it back, Gruber spoke up.

"Victor, is it absolutely necessary . . . I mean, do we really need to bring Simon in on this? Frankly, I'd like to take those fuckers out myself."

Kolnikov motioned for quiet.

"No. Not now . . . I'll . . . we'll discuss all that later." He turned back to Black. "Will you please take this up to Communications and have them get it out as quickly as possible?"

"I'll try, Commander. But there's been nothing but high-priority official traffic going out or in for the past two days."

"Well then, call me here if there's a snag. I'll handle it."

"Aye-aye, sir." Black started out the door. Kolnikov called after him.

"One more thing, Roger. Are these staterooms secure? I mean, are they anywhere near the W Division officers' area?"

"No, sir. Their staterooms are immediately adjacent to the entrance to the W Spaces on the second deck port side."

"Good."

"And one other thing, for what it's worth, Commander . . . they hardly ever leave that area, except for meals in the Wardroom. Otherwise, they stick strickly to themselves —real moles, sir."

"You don't say!" Victor grinned, resisting the desire to look at Gruber's and Lowell's faces. "That's good news. But do please hurry with that message."

FORTY-ONE

"REAL MOLES!" Victor sat back in the semi-darkness and chuckled to himself. He took off his cap, placed it on the desk, unbuttoned his jacket, and loosened his collar. Black's chance remark had given him his first respite from tension in over twelve hours. "But now we know where they live." He looked at Gruber and Lowell, his face all peasant slyness now.

Gruber had settled into the other chair. Lowell was lounging against one of the lockers. Kolnikov steepled his fingers in front of his nose and pondered silently for nearly a quarter hour. Gruber finally interrupted his meditation.

"So what do we do now?"

Kolnikov chewed on his lip for a few seconds before replying.

"What do we do, Max? We perform the time-honored Naval maneuver called 'hurry up and wait.' "

"Just wait?" Gruber shifted nervously in his chair. "I think we're making a mistake. If this is the Big Show they've been working on all these years, shouldn't we throw the switch on them as quickly as possible? We don't know their timetable."

"Granted, Max. But we can make an educated guess."

"Such as . . ."

"Such as it involves the nuclear weapons on this ship. That's point one. They've put too much time and effort into getting themselves on station here just to take a sightseeing trip. And it's not just simple espionage. The makeup and capabilities—and mission—of the supercarriers is pretty common knowledge."

"Excuse me, Victor," interjected Lowell, "but I've never been on one of these. What exactly is their mission?"

"Well . . . basically, Jon, a supercarrier has two missions—nuclear attack and tactical support of a fleet or an amphibious landing. The primary one is nuclear attack." Kolnikov shifted his chair around to face Lowell, who was now sitting on the lower bunk.

"The *Forrestal*, for example, carries about eighty-five aircraft, most of which are dual mission fighter-bombers, and some hundred tactical nuclear weapons. In the event of all-out war, her primary job is to deliver all those weapons onto preselected targets—in this case, targets in Bulgaria, southern Romania, and Hungary—the southern tier, so to speak, of the Warsaw Pact countries. Or, possibly in this case, against the divisions apparently being massed around Turkey." He pointed at Lowell. "Jon . . . you saw the way the planes were spotted on the deck yesterday, and again today? Well, from that spot pattern, they can launch the entire attack wave with every nuke on the ship in under seventeen minutes. In fact, that's all this whole thing has to survive; then the primary mission is accomplished and we're expendable—if she survives after that, every-thing else is pure gravy."

"Seventeen minutes . . . only that . . . and it's all over . . . all this for seventeen minutes."

"Or less, if they get us first. And you can be sure they'll be coming after us with every-thing they've got. That's why they try to shadow us as closely as possible. And you can be sure, if we try to launch, they'll be hitting us with all sorts of shit—planes, missiles, subs—anything to stop the launch. If the balloon goes up, Jon, you'll see the biggest Fourth of July show around this ship you've ever seen in your life."

"Then what are her chances?"

"Of getting off the full strike? Maybe fifty-fifty. Of surviving more than a half hour, next to zilch."

"You forgot one thing, Victor," interrupted Gruber. "If they have people *inside*—in this instance, Gelman and Company—they don't need to come after us. They could simply foul up the arming of the nukes and we'd send off the whole strike armed with a hundred fucking duds. That would allow them to con-centrate their whole defense on stopping whatever's coming at them from the land."

"Yes, Max. And that would mean we couldn't break up their formations if they do invade Turkey."

"What about the other supers? The article in the newspaper said that the *Enterprise* and *Nimitz* left the East Coast yesterday."

"It'll still be ten days at the minimum before they could get here. By then, the

Soviets could have control of half of the country, including the Dardanelles—Istanbul's less than seventy miles from the Bulgarian border. Our best chance—our only chance—to stop them is to hit them early, destroy their armored columns while they're still massed behind the border or bottled up in the valleys leading out of the Balkans. Once they spread out and get control of the towns and cities, it'll be too late for nuclear weapons to be effective, or even useable. We can't, for instance, bomb Istanbul; that'd be burning down the house to cook the roast. We'd be fucked, Max. They'd have control of every important point and we'd be forced to go in and dig them out piecemeal. It'd take fifty divisions. Impossible. It'd tie down every ground soldier we've got."

"What about the Turkish Army?"

"They'd put up a good fight, certainly. But they're faced with a two-front war. They can't concentrate everything on the Bulgarian front with another Red Army rolling across Turkey from the east practically unopposed. And for that matter, the entire Turkish Army could only *delay* a full-scale Soviet thrust; they're outnumbered, outgunned, outtanked. They couldn't hold more'n three days at the most before the other side flattened them."

"Christ! Then, we're it!"

"We're it, Max."

"Then I say we move now." Gruber was up and pacing.

"How?"

"By taking them out—now—ourselves. Stop them before they can pull it off."

"If that's their game, Max, they've already played their trump. Every nuke on this ship is already up on the Flight Deck slung under the planes. If they're misarmed, it would've been done down in the W Section before they went up the elevator. My guess is that right now we're sitting six decks below about *one hundred nuclear duds.*"

"Oh my God, Victor. Then, what do we do?"

"We wait to hear from Simon."

"But what if the Russians jump off before we hear from Simon?"

"I doubt they will, just yet." Victor looked as self-assured as an icon of a saint. Gruber was finding this complacency maddening.

"*C'mon*, Victor! I know you know the area, but what crystal ball tells you the Russians aren't stepping out this very minute?"

Kolnikov shook his head violently. "No crystal ball. But I do know that area . . . I've been there . . . you remember the time?" Gruber agreed. "Well, the newspaper article said that troops were massing across from Istanbul and the Gallipoli Peninsula. Right? But that other divisions were reported moving through Sofia to the west and were believed to be heading for the Yugoslav border. Right?"

Victor paused and looked around the room.

"No map here." He made a face. "Oh well . . . anyway, that's the wrong direction if they were planning to support a push east through Turkey. Besides, that makes no strategic sense. Look!" Kolnikov twisted sideways in his chair and raised his hands against an imaginary map in the air. "Turkey's here. One group of Russians are over here on the east." He stretched his right hand all the way out. "The others are back here. And this is the important part—the Dardanelles and the Aegean." He moved his left in a sweeping, circular motion. "Not only the straits, but the Aegean; they have to control that too—or keep us from controlling it. And the key to control of the Aegean is here—Salonika."

"But that's in Greece."

"Yes, and under fifty miles from the Bulgarian border, near Petrich—one day's dash by armored forces. Control of Salonika would give them the only major deepwater port north of Piraeus. With the Turkish Army split, we can figure two days—tops—to secure the Bosporus and Dardenelles. If, in those same two days, they can capture and secure Salonika—and the Greek Army is even *less* prepared to stop them—they can move their entire Black Sea Fleet down, and be operating out of there—at least partially—by day three or four."

Victor sat back and dropped his hands on his knees like a father who has just laid out the facts of life to his children. "There you have it. Secure access to the Mediterranean *and* a warm-water seaport and Naval base, all in one lightning stroke."

"But what about the Yugoslavian border?" Max still looked less than totally convinced of Kolnikov's logic. "Couldn't those divisions still be needed to guard it?"

"Against what, Max? Yugoslavia's shakier than warm Jello; no threat at all."

"Then, what about a strike across Yugoslavia? To Kotor or Dubrovnik on the Adriatic?"

"Not worth the trouble right now. That's two hundred and fifty miles straight across the worst stretch of the Balkans through Montenegro. No major roads and a half million Montenegran mountain men that'd make the Afghanis look like pygmies with peashooters. It'd take months. And what for? Without Salonika and control of the Aegean, they'd be worthless. *With* Salonika, they're in position to support the takeover of every Yugoslavian port from Kotor to Rijeka in the event of civil war there. No! I still say it's Salonika." He stopped to light a cigarette. "*And* . . . I say it'll be another two days because they have to bring those divisions another two hundred miles down the Valley of the Struma from Sofia. And with our nukes neutralized, they can take their own sweet time getting into position."

"And the *Enterprise* and *Nimitz* won't count?"

"Not in the least. They're four thousand miles from their most extreme launch point. It'll be all over before they even reach Gibraltar. By then, any land-launched capability will've been scrubbed by counter-strikes, and the carriers'll be sitting ducks practically the moment they pass Gibraltar—*if* they're allowed to get *that* far." Victor lifted his hands as if in benediction. "It's beautiful! With our nukes spiked, we're flattened. We probably won't even be able to hold Piraeus; we'll be forced back on Naples —and they'll have the whole Eastern Mediterranean—the Suez Canal, Cyprus, Greece, Turkey, Egypt—the whole Middle East . . . and *us*, gentlemen, by the short hairs!"

The enormity of the possibilities as Victor spun them out had made him increasingly agitated. His hands shook so violently that, when he tried to fetch another cigarette, he fumbled the pack halfway across the floor. Lowell darted down and fielded the bouncing pack, pulled a cigarette out, lit it, and reached it over to Kolnikov, who took it very carefully between his lips.

"Thanks, Jon." Victor sat back and let the curling smoke smooth out the wrinkles in his nervous system. Finally, Lowell, who had listened intently up to now, had a question.

"If all this was so easy, Victor, why didn't they do all this a long time ago?"

"Because of the attack carriers, Jon. They're the only launching platform flexible enough to move to where it's needed . . . without flying long distances over somebody else's air space, which might or might not be permitted."

"Then it's been *our* nukes that've kept them out—and only our nukes."

Victor stubbed out the half-smoked cigarette. "Exactly, Jon . . . until now. And that's why we went to prison. And why there's been only minor flaps involving

Counter Intelligence Section for nine years—
no *wonder* Simon's skittier'n a goddamn cat!
When nothing big—nothing important, goes
down for damn near ten years, there's *gotta*
be something really big building up."

"But why so long, Victor?"

"Because it had to be set up just right,
without a single hitch. They had to create
three identities—three complete Navy
careers—with every piece of background
material and supporting documents in the
right place in the right bureau—from
BUPERS to BUMED. Christ, I even noticed
in Stoddard's — Fisher's, rather—Medical
Record that he had VD back in 1974 while
serving aboard this ship. It's the most
thorough job of creation since the Creation
itself."

"It's hard to believe, Victor."

"Not really, Jon. Not if you know the
Russians and how they think. They're chess
players—in more dimensions than most of us
can imagine. Shit! This was probably con-
jured up over twenty years ago as a contin-
gency plan by some genius in Soviet Strategic
Planning."

"That's scary, Victor."

"What scares me more is that they pulled it
off. At least this far. Now they've got the right
incident, the right moment in our global
position, and the right men in the right
place."

"And a hundred duds on the Flight Deck,"
reiterated Gruber. "And I say we do something now—while we know the picture and
they haven't moved yet."

Kolnikov was about to answer when Lowell suddenly jumped out of the bunk. "Victor! What about those catapults we heard when we came in? Maybe they've launched *already!*" Lowell's eyes were wide with sudden apprehension.

"Don't worry, Jon. That was just the Combat Air Patrol going off the spare Cat. If that'd been the full Emergency launch, you'd've thought you were in San Francisco during the Great Quake!" Mollfied, Lowell sat down again.

Gruber was pacing again. "I wish you hadn't given Black his gun back."

"Why?"

"So we could take 'em out ourselves if we have to."

"And accomplish what, Max? We don't know how to rearm those bombs or what they did to them. For all we know, they could be completely wrecked inside."

"Then let's go to the Captain."

"With what? With ID cards that say we're Supply—not Intelligence? With the phony Audit orders? Do we say, 'Captain, we came aboard your ship to rob it, but now want to save it from a band of desperate saboteurs who are posing as your W Division officers?' And if he believes that, what does he do? He checks. And he could check for a month and wind up right back from where he started . . . because these people—Hartranft, Dyer, and Fisher—are real . . . *real*, Max, *real* . . . realer even than you and I and Lowell by a nine-year longshot." Kolnikov stood up and put his hand on Gruber's shoulders to stop his

216

pacing. "You know where they'd put us, Max? Right in the rubber room. No! We *have* to wait for Simon's reply—and I hope to Christ he's gotten the message. Maybe I should've sent one to New York as well."

"What if Simon knows about this operation?"

"I doubt it, Max. It would've made no sense for him to spring us as decoys if he knew they had already flown the coop and were over here. They beat him to the punch."

"Either that or he's after whoever's higher up running the show and is trying to flush *them* with us. In which case he'd have this operation covered and ready to take out the minute the big boys break cover."

"Good thinking, Max. And all the more reason we have to sit tight. Simon said he was going out on a yardarm. We can't shake it under him now."

"I agree. Hurry up and fucking wait!"

Suddenly a loud knock on the door froze everybody in place. The knock came again. Gruber instinctively slipped over to the side of the door. Lowell scrambled after him. After the third knock, Kolnikov spoke.

"Yes, who is it?"

"The Wardroom Officer."

Victor let out a long sigh of relief and opened the door. A tall, lanky redhead with a look of eternally ironic amusement on his ruddy face stepped in. A pile of towels rested over his arm.

"I'm Lieutenant JG Schermerhorn. Roger Black asked me to take care of you, and I thought it'd be better for me to come than to send a steward—they talk, you know." He laid the towels on the unlighted desk and opened the satchel he carried in his other hand. "I brought you some sandwiches, some cakes, cups, and a thermos of hot coffee . . . I . . ."

"Lieutenant, you have saved our lives!" cried Kolnikov.

Without acknowledging Victor's elation, the tall officer reached into the pocket of his blue windbreaker and produced a litre bottle of Spanish brandy. "It's the only thing I have over in my room," he began apologetically, "but Roger said you had a rough trip."

"No, you have not saved our lives," blurted Kolnikov. "You have just made us die and go to heaven. *Thank* you, Comrade."

FORTY-TWO

THE PARTIALLY emptied brandy bottle, its cork slightly awry, stood well back in a niche of the desk as Kolnikov sat eating, its illicit contents discreetly hidden from the doorway. All forms of alcoholic beverage are strictly *verboten* on US Navy vessels, though it is an open secret that the rule, introduced in 1916 by President Wilson's frantically prohibitionist Secretary of the Navy, Josephus Daniels, is observed more in the breach by nearly all hands. Nevertheless, strongly inculcated habits persist, and Victor had treated it like a pack of cigarettes passed about between small boys gathered for a furtive smoke in the attic.

Lieutenant Schermerhorn's sandwiches, coffee, and brandy, followed by a brief attempt at napping—Gruber and Lowell on the bunks; Kolnikov, by his insistance, in the chair by the desk with his feet up—had refreshed and relaxed them somewhat. Now they turned to the dinner Black had smuggled to them, digesting it silently along with the growing awareness of the incredible facts of their new situation.

Without a word, Gruber lifted his empty glass and held it over next to Victor, who uncorked the bottle and poured a carefully tiny measure.

"We have to conserve, Max—this *and* our

wits." He looked over at Lowell, who sat on the edge of the lower bunk balancing his plate on his knees. "Some more for you?" Lowell shook his head.

They went back to eating, each absorbed in his own thoughts.

The sound of a bosun's pipe drifted in from the passageway outside. "NOW HEAR THIS. THE MOVIE IN THE WARDROOM WILL BE: THE POSTMAN ALWAYS RINGS TWICE. THE MOVIE ON HANGAR DECK WILL BE: THE EMPIRE STRIKES BACK."

"Hardly first-run stuff," Gruber commented absentmindedly over his glass.

Victor finished a sip of his coffee and put the cup down. "Still an improvement over my day. All we ever got were what they called 'sea prints,' usually with Francis X. Bushman playing the ingenue. At least the bosun's mate got the titles right." He paused to add some brandy to his own glass. "Did I ever tell you about he time the bosun's mate passed the word, 'THE MOVIE IN THE WARDROOM WILL BE KING HENRY THE VEE-AYE-AYE-AYE'?"

Gruber half laughed. "No. But you did tell me about the one who passed the word, 'NOW KNOCK OFF ALL PROFANE AND OBSCENE LANGUAGE ABOUT THE DECKS—THERE'S *CUNT* ABOARD!' Did that really happen while you were here?"

Victor slid back in his chair. "Not really. But it did happen somewhere, sometime—you can be sure of that. It just makes for better telling when it's in the first person; sea stories are never told in the third person. It always happened on *your* ship, preferably on *your* watch; makes them more . . . uh . . . vivid . . . also funnier when some boot ensign tries to tell you some story that was old when John Paul Jones was a midshipman." Warmed by the brandy, Victor began to ramble off into yet another anecdote of the kind sailors tell each other to pass the dead-slow passage of time at sea. Suddenly there was a knock on the door. It was Roger Black. He was carrying an official-looking briefcase.

"Did you have any trouble?" queried Victor as he turned the lock behind the youthful officer.

"No, sir. There was only one person in the office, the Duty Yeoman, and he was busy typing up papers. He didn't see me take anything, and just for good measure I locked the file drawer—with one of my own locks. Anybody wanting to get in will have to go to a heckuva lot of trouble, so I think we're safe."

The young man smiled, obviously pleased with himself. Victor relaxed another notch internally. Good! Black was in with all four feet—even proud of his little bit of cloak-and-dagger thinking with the lock. No more fear that he'd have second thoughts and maybe go to the Captain or Exec. Blessed relief!

Black slipped three bulky manila folders out of the case, all looking as if they had been beating about from ship to shore station as long as the subjects of each had been in the Navy. No question about it: the job was perfect to the slightest detail. He handed them over to Victor, then stood expectantly, shifting on his feet deferentially. The big man looked up.

"I guess," mused Victor, "you're curious—right?"

Black nodded.

"All right, then." Victor motioned Black further in to the room. "The very least we owe you is some explanation of what we're getting you into—especially since we nearly got you into one mess."

The young man made himself as comfortable as possible against a locker while Kolnikov, as succinctly as possible, retailed the whole story to him. Only an occasional, barely believing shake of the head revealed the natural amazement of the Supply type at the twists and turns of the labyrinthine Byzantium which is Intelligence.

"And that's where we are at the moment," concluded Kolnikov, with a spread of his huge hands. "And that's why we have to cool our heels here until we get word from Roschestvensky." Victor reached for the brandy bottle and began pouring for the other three. As if his memory were jigged by the sight, Black gave a start and commenced digging in his briefcase, finally producing a fifth of scotch from the bottom.

"Here. I forgot this . . . Mike . . . er, Lieutenant Schermerhorn sent this."

Victor took the bottle and held it admiringly. "My compliments to the Lieutenant—a true officer and gentleman." He looked up at Black. "Will you join us?"

"No thank you, sir. I don't drink. And I should go, if you will excuse me."

"Certainly. And my thanks for the files."

As Black reached for the door handle, Victor held up a finger. "One more favor, if you will. Would you take a wander past Communications—just to make sure our message went out?"

"Will do, sir." He paused; he was still digesting. He turned back. "You're absolutely certain? Hartranft, Dyer, and Fisher?"

Victor nodded firmly. "They seemed decent enough to me."

With a final shake of his head, he was gone.

FORTY-THREE

"GOD, SHE'S BIG!"

Lowell stood in the blue-gray shadows of dawn in the Straits of Messina and swept his eyes across the seemingly endless carpet of the *Forrestal*'s Flight Deck.

"Four and a half *acres* of two-inch armored steel." Victor swept his arm in the same arc as Lowell's eyes, like an Armenian rug merchant making a point of sale.

"And those links of the anchor chain—do they really weigh three hundred and sixty pounds apiece?"

"And each chain is nearly a half mile long, and connected to a thirty-ton anchor." Victor was in the mood to impress. This had been his ship for nearly two years as a young Ensign, and he had never really gotten over the magnificence of her.

"In fact . . . let me tell you about what happened on the *Saratoga* one time. While on her way back across the Atlantic—in a storm one night—the pelican hook gave way. And the anchor payed out into the Atlantic—at that point some two miles down. And when the bitter end of that anchor chain came out of the chain locker, it slashed the foc'sle—*and that two-inch Flight Deck*—like a bullwhip in *a cardboard carton!*"

Lowell gave a shudder of vicarious recognition. They had just emerged from the massive forecastle by way of a small hatch onto the starboard catwalk forward of the superstructure.

The planes were arranged as they had first seen them in the Gulf of Naples—obediently lined up behind their respective catapults, each with one or more blunt white shapes slung under them. Marine sentries mother-henned each one, as if the bloated chrysalises would produce young at any moment.

The only former carrier sailor of the three, Kolnikov led his charges along the catwalk like a cruise director conducting a couple of landlubber dowagers through the Grand Salon.

Though the sun had broken the eastern horizon by an hour, it had not achieved the heights of the mountain ridge to their left as the *Forrestal* daintily tested the waters of the straits at a chaste ten knots. Deep blue shadows engulfed the great ship as she threaded her way into the steep, narrow gorge ahead.

Kolnikov explained:

"The Straits of Messina—between Italy proper and Sicily—is just about the hairiest passage in the world—next to the Straits of Shimonoseki in Japan—due to differential currents. You have to go through *exactly* at neap tide; otherwise you risk whirlpools that can take a destroyer and turn her around where she was coming from—literally!"

"Then why go this way?"

"Because it's faster." Victor looked at his watch. "Even with slowing down by two hours, it's better to wait for the tide here than to go around Sicily—by at least six hours' steaming.

Lowell turned himself slowly, drinking in the grandeur of the mountains—almost black to the left, sunstruck and tinted to the west—and the majestic grey leviathan which was slipping silently between their embrace. Something ahead caught his eye.

"Victor. Those wires up ahead. Can we clear them?"

"Just barely. At this time of day, at least. But we couldn't once the sun goes to work on them later on. The *Saratoga* found that out back in 1961—went through in the early afternoon and the top of her mast took down a couple of them. The *Sara* always seemed to be prone to freak accidents—like that, and the anchor giving way. A friend of mine who was aboard at the time said it was quite a show, scared the shit out of them *and* the Italians."

"Then why are they there?"

"That, Jon, is the entire electric power supply for all of eastern Sicily. Fuel's so expensive—even was back then—that the Italians built power lines the whole length of the country from their hydroelectric dams up North in the Italian Alps, sort of an Italian TVA."

All three watched in silence as the slender black wires, slung between the opposing mountaintops like a hammock, approached the ship; and followed them with their eyes as they cleared the towering mast, it seemed, by barely inches. The spell finally broken, the three men started moving aft.

"Is it safe for us to be up here?" said Lowell in a low, conspiratorial voice.

"Fairly safe. Right now, at least. Gelman and his boys are probably still in the sack. It's not even reveille for another ten minutes or so. And, the most they might do is come up for an inspection—just for show." Victor snorted. "Just for show! What is there to inspect on a dud? Just keep one eye on the hatches out of the superstructure. That's where they'll come from."

They moved slowly aft. The Marine sentry guarding the first plane in line, an F4H Phantom II, came to attention and saluted Victor. He returned it with a smile and a "good morning," as if being an officer and gentleman again made it so.

"You know, Jon . . . it's a shame you've spent seventy-five percent of your Naval career, so far, in the slammer. " Lowell winced. "Because . . . actually, Jon, I think you would've enjoyed sea duty on something like this. I know I did." He stopped and confronted Lowell. "What *are* your plans now?"

Lowell hesitated. "I don't know. I guess I'll just go home for awhile. Maybe go back to Harvard and study law, if they'll let me in."

"What about you, Max?"

"I'll go back into Intelligence, most likely. What about you?"

Victor turned and clamped his hands firmly down on the rail, rocking back and forth on his feet as he alternately thought and spoke.

"Well . . . actually, Max . . . I don't know. Eighteen hours ago, I was planning to be a millionaire in Brazil. Now, I don't know. But I doubt it'll be the Navy anymore."

"Why not? You're one of the best analysts they ever had."

"Back then, I was, Max. Back then."

"I suppose you were just bullshitting when you laid out the whole thing yesterday? Christ, Victor, you can think rings around the whole crew!"

"It didn't save us nine years ago—did it, Max?" Gruber lapsed into silence. Lowell was admiring the plane behind them.

"Victor . . . how quickly could they launch the first plane?" Kolnikov stepped over to the edge of the Flight Deck. He started pointing around the deck.

"See those wisps of steam, Jon? That means the Cat is 'hot,' that she's got steam up, ready to fire. Actually, the Cats are one of the most fascinating features of the whole ship. They're shaped like a double-barreled shotgun, except with ports to let in more steam every few yards along its length. The 'shuttle'—which is like a slug in the barrel—carries the hook. See where the plane's connected by that cable to the nose? And see that other connection; back aft by the tail? That's actually a breakable metal connection. When they give her the steam, the connection breaks, releasing the plane. It's actually like a giant slingshot." Victor demonstrated. "Except that the plane is accelerated to a hundred fifty knots in just under three hundred feet." His arm followed the swoop of the imaginary plane off the deck.

"Then comes the most interesting part:

they stop the shuttle—which weighs twenty-five hundred pounds and is traveling at a hundred fifty knots—in just *five feet!*"

"*Five feet!* How?"

"By ingenuity, son—ingenuity. There's a spring-loaded, spade-shaped affair underneath the shuttle—called a 'plow'—which, at the end of the run, drops down into a tank of water. Stops the whole bloody mess in five feet—in fact, that's the jolt you felt each time the Cats fired."

Lowell shook his head in awe. Kolnikov steered him over to a bank of controls just under the edge of the deck.

"These are the controls. When the Launching Officer gives the signal, the controller, here, turns the safety crank to 'Fire' and pushes this button, there. And off she goes!"

"Could you fire her now?"

"Yes, Jon. But, I think it might upset the sentry. Also, without a pilot, she'd dump into the drink with the goddamnedest splash you ever saw." Victor paused to collect a memory. "I saw them do it once. In Bremerton Shipyard. With a contraption they call a dummy load; to test the Cats after they've rebuilt them to see if their terminal velocities are right. Right off the bow! Then, you wait for what seems forever. Then she hits! Sounds like a sixteen-inch shell hitting the water, except that the splash is about four times as high as a shell—almost as high as the superstructure. Or that's what it looks like."

"Jesus!" Lowell shook the image out of his head.

They were just forward of the looming superstructure now. And they could see the faces of the bridge watch peering down at them.

Gruber tapped Kolnikov lightly on the arm. "Victor," he queried, "didn't you tell us, once, that you were aboard *Forrestal* during the Cuban Missile Crisis in 1962?"

Victor brightened to the memory; he leaned back against the catwalk rail. "Yes. We were visiting Genoa at the time—great town, Genoa. Hooked up with an absolutely fantastic *italiana*, an exotic dancer at the Caprice Club. Jesus, what a woman! Followed the ship around for the rest of the tour, wanted me to marry her and bent every luscious bone in her body to convince me I should." Kolnikov paused for a minute to savor the thought of that long-past passion; his special weakness was Mediterranean women, and she was one of the best he had known—second only to his Tina. Then, like someone coming out of a pleasant dream, he continued.

"They pulled us out in the middle of the afternoon—just before liberty call. *Damn!* Just like they did yesterday in Naples, except that we weren't at standby readiness or even anything like it. What a Chinese fire drill that was! In less than three hours, we were steaming on station with everything up on deck like it is now, listening to Kennedy's speech, waiting for the final whistle to blow, and feeling very big and conspicuous, even out in all that open ocean. And . . ." He paused for effect. "You know what the movie was in the wardroom that night?" He regarded Gruber and Lowell quizically; both shook their heads.

"*On The Beach!* There we were, sitting only four decks below a hundred armed nukes, with all the aircrews suited up, briefed and lounging in their ready rooms waiting to go . . . and we're watching a movie about the end of the human race as a result of what we were standing by ready to do." Victor closed his eyes and shuddered his shoulders; the other two stood in transfixed silence. "And . . . and when the lights came on at the end . . . you never saw such a crew of pasty-faced men in your life . . . one commander with enough metal on his chest to sink a battleship was sitting there absolutely shaking, tears streaming down his face . . . practically bawling like a baby—not from fear, mind you, but from the thought of what we might be about to do. We *all* sat there—totally stunned."

"What happened then?" interjected Lowell, his still-youthful countenance lined with curious concern.

"Finally, the Exec turned to the Navigator and growled, 'Who's the movie officer, tonight—*Admiral Gorchkov?*' That sort of broke up the ice, but not completely. Instead of staying around to play cards and acey-deucey, most everybody just filed out in silence. I went down and wrote a last letter to my parents . . . sort of spooky, though—writing a letter you know might never even get off the ship . . . or be delivered . . . or find no one alive to read it when it did arrive. Father O'Neill held a special Mass on the hangar deck that night and half the crew was there—every man who wasn't on watch or had a job to do; Protestant, Catholics, Jews, they were all there." Kolnikov sniffed, stiffened, then started moving aft, speaking thoughtfully as he went. "And to this day, I can't bring myself to sing 'Waltzing Matilda'; even hearing it makes me choke up."

Victor tipped his cap over his eyes and led them briskly around the catwalk outboard of the looming superstructure, past the giant mobile aircraft crane parked next to the Number 4 elevator. "They call that the 'cherry picker,' " Victor mentioned as they passed it. "If a plane crashes on landing and they can't move it any other way—especially if it's on fire—they just pick it up and dump it overboard, just like that." His arm made a sweeping motion over his head, ending with his finger pointing at the still-dark sea eighty feet below them.

As they reached the landing area, Gruber studied the four heavy cables stretched taut athwart the deck. "How do those things actually stop the aircraft?" he asked.

Victor pointed toward the tail of a nearby plane, a long, sleek F8 Chance-Vought Crusader. "See that tailhook? When they head in on their final approach, the pilot drops it down—the curved end is also called a 'plow.' As you can see, the cables are held slightly above the level of the deck by those spring strips; the wheels roll over them, but the plow slips under and catches, stopping the plane in . . . about . . . three hundred or so feet. The cables are set for each plane; that is,

232

each pilot radios in his fuel state to Primary Flight Control—PRI-FLY—up there." He directed their gaze to a structure which resembled an airport control tower perched high above them on the after end of the island. "They punch in the weight of fuel and the type of plane on their console, and that automatically sets the control valves on the hydraulic pistons down below."

Gruber grinned. "And what if there's a malfuction, or somebody goofs?"

"Then you have problems. Too little tension and you could theoretically have a heavy plane dangling off the end of the angle by its tailhook; too much on a light plane and you'll tear its whole tail off."

"Sounds hairy," commented Lowell, shaking his head.

"It is. In the two years I was aboard, we lost eighteen men—all but one of them either airdales or Flight Deck crew."

"Flight Deck crew as well?"

Victor nodded. "The most dangerous peacetime job in the Navy, after flying itself. See those knuckle bolts that join the cables just beyond where they come up through those pullies from down below? Well, the part that actually crosses the deck is called the 'cross-deck pendant'; they're joined like that so they can be replaced when they wear without restringing the entire system—and if they break, it's usually that joint and not the pendant itself. And when one of them does let go—and they do, from time to time—the whole mess 'wipes the clock,' as they say."

"What about the people back here?"

queried Lowell, his eyes apprehensively surveying an area where a lot of people obviously had to be working during landings.

"Just before each plane touches down, everybody back here ducks below the level of the Flight Deck."

Lowell breathed a sigh of relief. Gruber, apparently unconcerned with the fate of Flight Deck crews, had been studying a plane's tailhook. "Victor," he interposed, "how does the plane unhook after it stops?"

"Usually . . . when the plane stops . . . it's dipped forward on its nose from the stop, and when it rights itself, it rolls back a little; the pilot then retracts the hook and taxis forward out of the way of the next incoming plane—which, incidentally, when an Air Group is fully worked up to a maximum operational peak, is only seventeen seconds behind him."

"And if his hook doesn't fall free?"

"The 'Tailhook Johnny'—he's usually the youngest, fastest, bravest, and dumbest kid on the Flight Deck crew—runs out from his protective enclosure aft of the island with a thing that looks like a short, double-ended crow bar and unhooks the wire—all the while ducking jet blast from other planes, whirling props, and wings swinging all around him. Then he gives the pilot the thumbs-up and dashes back to safely until the next time. Oh, yes! *And* all the while *also* hoping the plane that's only three hundred yards aft by now has caught the wave-off from the Landing Officer."

"Jesus!" muttered Gruber.

"Of course, it doesn't always turn out that way," added Kolnikov, warming to his subject and an entranced audience. "Once . . . when I was aboard . . . an A3D Skywarrior— they were the heaviest thing that ever flew regularly off a flight deck, twin jet medium-range bombers that weighed seventy thousand pounds *dry*—broke a wire. But not the cross-deck pendant; he broke the purchase cable deep down inside the arresting machinery. Of course it didn't stop him, and he put on full power to fly on off the angle. But as he did, three hundred feet of one-inch cable rove through this hook and, as he cleared the angle, the bitter end came free —miracle it didn't cut off his tail—and went snapping back across the deck like a mammoth bullwhip . . . hit some crew up for'ard where they weren't expecting that kind of trouble; cut a Chief's head off, cut another man in two, and took both legs off another. And that wasn't the wildest part! The Tailhook Johnny had mistakenly run out on deck, only to find himself trapped out there with this thing coming at him. If he panicked and ran, he was done for—head, legs, or middle for sure. But he didn't; he had the presence of mind to stand there and judge the uncoming wire, deciding to jump or duck. He jumped, and the wire clipped under both his feet, tumbling him down hard on the deck. Except for some scrapes and bruises, he was all right—but he had nothing but uppers on both shoes; the wire had shaved off the soles and heels clean as a whistle."

Victor stopped for a break. Gruber sucked

in a whistle through his teeth. "I'd say he was one Tailhook Johnny who wasn't so dumb."

"He had some dumb luck, though. And you need that here. One kid I knew wasn't so lucky. He was driving a 'mule' towing a plane. He was looking back to make sure he didn't run the plane into anything and drove himself straight into a propeller—it shredded him from the waist up, and spattered the pieces like bloody hamburger down half the deck."

Lowell was starting to look pale; Gruber was merely fascinated. Kolnikov continued.

"That's why nobody—*nobody*—who doesn't work or belong on the Flight Deck goes there during Flight Ops. In fact, the first thing they do with new arrivals is show them a movie of one gory accident after another— a lot of them filmed during World War Two and Korea—after which, let me tell you, you're a *believer!*"

Lowell shrugged and shook his head. "I don't think I'd like to be stationed on a carrier—not if it's like that."

Victor patted his shoulder. "Don't worry. It's not like that all the time. A carrier— especially a supercarrier—is still the most interesting ship you could ever be on—most sea duty is deadly boring, actually. On a carrier, not only do you have all the comforts of a Cunard Liner practically, anytime you get bored you can go up there"—Victor indicated several levels of open catwalk sur-rounding the island—"to Vultures' Row and watch the Greatest Three-Ring Show On Earth—makes Ringling Brothers, Barnum and Bailey look like a WCTU teaparty."

Gruber broke into a sardonic laugh. "Did you say 'Vultures' Row,' Victor?"

"That's what they call it, Max."

They had nearly reached the stern by now. And the great steel leviathan had achieved the open sea. Free of the strictures of close passage, she responded like a liberated colt. Under their feet, the three men felt the rising rumble as four forty-ton bronze screws bit into blue water with the force of a third of a million horsepower, felt her heel slightly, majestically to starboard as she swung left— eastward toward Greece.

Just then, they heard the sound of gunfire coming from close by their position on the ship's broad stern. Gruber and Lowell started. Kolnikov retained his composure.

"Shotguns!" he announced, chuckling at his companions' ignorance of the great ship's many amenities. "There's a skeeter on the fantail. When we're not recovering aircraft, it's one of the most popular places aboard." (Victor smiled at he use of "we"—as if he had suddenly been transported back nearly twenty years, was still a proud part of *Forrestal*, and was showing her off—which he was, with a touch of pride that had survived all that had transpired in between.) The two men relaxed, only to be jolted anew by the unmistakable sound of automatic weapons fire. Both stared at Victor questioningly.

Victor grinned. "Thompsons. They're much more fun than shotguns."

The ship had seemed to come alive with the new course and speed. A bosun's pipe shrilled through the clear morning air, followed by the call to "Morning Quarters." Like souls summoned from their graves by the Trumpet of Judgment, men in dull blue denim work uniforms appeared in great numbers, scurrying towards their appointed stations.

"I think we'd better go below," stated Kolnikov, looking about. "We've pressed our luck far enough."

As they headed forward toward the hatch from which they had emerged, Gruber pressed the question which had been bothering him since yesterday upon Kolnikov.

"Why haven't we heard from Simon, Victor? It's been over fourteen hours."

"I don't know. I'll check with Communications later. Maybe he's off somewhere else and didn't get the message in Washington. How do I know where he is?"

"But what if he doesn't get the message?" insisted Gruber. "What do we do then?"

"*I don't know, Max!* I'm not God Almighty." Kolnikov threw up his hands. "I'll give him another twenty-four hours. Then we'll decide."

"Decide what, Victor?"

"I don't know that either, Max. Without Simon, we're only three people throwing rocks at a black cat over the fence at midnight. I'm only guessing at Gelman's intentions. I'm only guessing at the whole business. You tell *me* what to do, Max. Can you?"

Gruber didn't answer. He ducked into the low hatch back into the forecastle. Lowell followed.

Victor stopped for a last, fugitive glance at a world still at peace with itself and everybody else. The street lights in nearby Messina had winked out; and people—intent on making the best of the coming day—must certainly be abroad, though it was too far to see them.

Fat, dumpy Sicilian widows, sheathed in a traditional funereal black—as if any other color would liberate their bursting sexuality to the detriment of the time-honored order of things—were already at their business of haggling with fishermen in fishwife voices which a thousand years of natural selection had honed to an edge designed to reduce even the most determined male to a state of abject submission. Just turn off that voice! Yes! I'll let you have these lampreys for your price, though I braved the furies of the sea. Take them! I can't abide the furies of the land.

The civil servants would be up soon too. Only the rich and the Honored Society would sleep late. Their revenues were secured.

Victor thought now about his mother and father. As good *Ukrainskye orthodoxniki*, they had cursed the Communists for the atheists they professed to be—with their desecration of the churches and holy places, their public spitting on the holy icons.

Still. Were they so wrong, these determined iconoclasts? They gave the land back to the people—or said they did. It was no longer possible for a noble to set his lanky borzoi on the innocent child of a *kulak* who had accidentally injured the aristocrat's prize horse—tearing apart the screaming child as

239

his own father looked on, made impotent with fear for his life and the lives of the rest of his family.

But then, the new masters had instituted new rules—and new ways to cow the people they had promised to free. So what was the difference? Were the thieves of Naples less reprehensible than the corporate thieves of Milan, who do their thieving wholesale? Wasn't it better to be stolen from face to face? At least you could confront the thief on the spot. Who do you remonstrate with when the package says "seven and twenty-three sixty-fourths ounces"? The American tourists who rave at the waiter over a paltry hundred lire on the *conto* go back to the Land of the Free and take their licks at the supermarket without a whimper—because they *trust* each other!

Free? Yes. Free. Free to get ripped off by the corporations. Just like the people in Russia and the rest of her colonies get ripped off by the State. The only difference is you get a little more for your money because the capitalists has to bust his ass to keep ahead of the other fellow who's out to get their first with the most for the least.

Victor shrugged. That side of human endeavor was beyond him. Right now he had a problem. Since he wasn't about to be a millionaire in Brazil, he hoped to God that Simon Roschestvensky would get the word— and tell him what the fuck to do.

Time *was* getting short.

FORTY-FOUR

"NOT A thing, Commander."

The Communications Watch Officer conscientiously went through the thick stack of messages on the board marked "Incoming" again, scrutinizing each one.

"No, sir. Not a thing." He shook his head slowly and looked around as if to see whether something wasn't missed.

"Are you absolutely certain it went out?"

"Absolutely, Commander. Here it is. Right in the log. Date time number 041522Z PRIORITY to Captain Simon Roschestvensky ONI-COUNTERINTEL WASHINGTON." He spun the heavy ledger book around for Kolnikov to inspect it himself.

"Very well. Thank you, Lieutenant."

"You're welcome, Commander. I'll keep an eye out and phone you the minute we get anything. Do we have your number?"

"No. But it's two-seven-seven."

The Lieutenant wrote it down on his watch scoop sheet. The Navy clock on the bulkhead across the teletype room said 0200. Victor turned and strolled slowly away down the passageway toward the hatch to the Flight Deck catwalk. Unable to sleep, he had been prowling about the less-populated parts of the ship keeping a sharp weather eye out for any unwanted meetings.

He cursed silently to himself. "Damn!

Thirty-three hours—and *nothing!* Why didn't I send that other message to New York as well?" He stopped and turned. Maybe he should now—anything to get through. Maybe even Tina. He turned back. If he hadn't heard by now, he couldn't possibly hear before morning. By then he'd have no choice but to act himself. Damn Simon! He was probably taking the weekend off. It'd be Monday morning before he got it now. Nothing to do but act. But how?

He undogged the hatch, stepped out into the blackness of the catwalk, and closed and redogged the hatch. As he waited for his eyes to adjust to the darkness, one of the sentries came over to check him out.

"Oh . . . Good evening, sir."

Victor returned his salute. "Good evening . . . just came up for some fresh air. Couldn't sleep."

"If you'd care to trade places with me, sir . . ."

Victor smiled and drifted forward aimlessly along the catwalk. The air was cold and there was no moon, but the thick carpet of stars in the crystal-black Aegean sky nevertheless made everything stand out sharply like a painting. It was deep night still. Victor looked out over the black ocean.

Kritikon Pelagos! The Sea of Crete. Entrance to the Aegean and grave of countless Naval warriors since before the time of Pericles. Now only a few single white lights of solitary night fishermen—and the world's largest engine of death and destruction—marked its placid surface.

Victor concentrated on the lights of a town reflecting across the water from what could be only ten miles away to the North. That would be Kithira, off the southern tip of the Peloponnesus. They'd be in Piraeus, in the shadow of Athens, by daylight. But why so many lights on over there? The frugal Greeks usually make do with a bare bulb streetlight or two at this hour. But now it looked as if every house in the town were ablaze. Suddenly a dry crackle like automatic weapons fire drifted across the silent deeps.

Not gunfire! Firecrackers! It was two hours past midnight on Easter Sunday morning—the Orthodox date coincided with the Roman this year. And all the Kithira, disgorging from Midnight Mass, was breaking the long Lenton Fast in a Dionysian explosion of food, drink, music, and fireworks. Victor listened hard for the sound of the music, but it was too far away. He stood there for a long while as the joyously celebrating town slid slowly away behind them. *Cristos anasti!* Christ is Risen. *Alithos anesti!* He is Risen, indeed! Without even being aware of it, Victor crossed himself.

The scene had lightened his spirits, if not his mind.

He had reached an outside ladder to the Hangar Deck. As he made his way down the successive flights, he discerned another officer standing against the rail at the bottom, his gaze fixed as Victor's had been on the twinkling town. As Victor drew closer, he made out the details of the tall, slender form which grew more unmistakable with each step he took. By now, the four gold stripes on the sleeves stood out like bracelets on a Nubian's arm. There was no mistaking the stance—or the man.

It was Simon Roschestvensky!

FORTY-FIVE

"WHERE THE Hell have you been, Simon?"

"Where have *you* been? I got here late this afternoon, and I've been looking high and low for you ever since. You didn't tell me in your message how to find you. Where've you been?"

"Lying low—waiting for a message from you."

"Damn!" Roschestvensky looked around quickly, then drew Victor over toward the rail. "Now tell me—what's the situation? How did you get here? And how did you find out about *them?*"

"One thing at a time. I'll tell you how I got here later. The important thing is that Gelman is the W Division Officer here and Horn and Stoddard are his assistants—all under aliases, complete with phony service records, clearances, the works! And my guess is that they've neutralized—misarmed, or whatever—every nuclear weapon on the ship." Victor quickly summarized the analysis he had delivered earlier to Gruber and Lowell. When he finished, Roschestvensky was silent for a long while, then turned to Victor.

"And before *Enterprise* or *Nimitz* can be brought to bear, we're blown out of the whole ballpark east of Italy. Well one thing's certain, Victor: nine years in the hole and you're just as sharp as ever. It's a masterful assessment; I couldn't think of a more logical —or potentially disastrous—scenario." He straightened up and backed away from the rail. "Now we've got to act, and act fast. Have you been in contact with anybody aboard about this?"

"Nobody. I wanted you in the picture before we did anything."

"What's the CO's name?"

"I don't know," replied Kolnikov with a touch of embarrassment.

"Well, that's the first place to start, then the Admiral. Come with me." Simon spun and bolted across the sponson into the cavernous gloom of the Hangar Deck with Victor hurrying to keep up with his sweeping strides. Roschestvensky convoyed them across the Hangar Deck to a ladder leading down to the second deck, then a short distance along the corridor to a door marked "Intelligence." Simon tried the door. It was locked. He knocked. No answer.

"Let's try over here."

The Public Information Office was open, but empty. Simon turned on the light.

"Good! This'll do."

"For what, Simon?"

"We'll use this until I can locate the Intelligence Officer—after I talk to the Old Man and the Admiral, neither of whom I relish waking at this hour. What's the telephone number here?" Roschestvensky checked the phone, then motioned Victor to take a seat at the desk.

"Victor, I want you to stay here by this

phone. Don't leave it for a minute. I'm going to get the brass alerted to what's going on. Then we'll work from there. If you're right, and all those weapons are neutralized, we're in deep trouble. We'll have to pry Gelman and his gang loose without their being able to sound the alarm. And in the meantime, find the nearest nuke experts and rush them in. If we're lucky, whatever they did can be corrected." Simon looked more genuinely worried than Victor had ever remembered seeing him. "If not . . . God, I hope we can do it in time!" He headed for the door. Halfway out he halted and leaned back in. "You did say Gruber and Lowell were with you. Are they safe?"

"Yes. They're in the Disbursing Officer's stateroom. That's where we've holed up."

"The *Disbursing* Officer? How . . ."

"I'll explain it all later."

"What's their phone number, there?"

"Uh . . . two-seven-seven."

"They aren't anywhere near the others, are they?"

"No. On the opposite side—three, one thirty-eight, one." Victor rattled off the location number: the shipboard equivalent of street number, apartment number, and Zip Code.

"Okay. Wait here. As soon as I get the Captain and Flag in gear, I'll call. So wait here. I don't want you wandering around and running into Gelman—not now." He closed his eyes and shook his head as if the consequences were too terrible to contemplate. Then, he closed the door behind him.

FORTY-SIX

VICTOR TRIED to make himself comfortable in the cramped, two-by-four cubicle alloted to the Public Information Officer and his staff. Simon's arrival had relaxed him, and now he was indescribably tired.

There wasn't really enough room to stretch out on the floor between the close-packed desks and files. He put his feet up and leaned back with his eyes closed, his cap bill pulled down to shade them from the light overhead.

No good. He reached up and switched off the light.

Still no good. He just couldn't sleep. He sat up, fumbled in the dark for the desk light, switched it on, and rummaged around the desk for something to read. A half dozen magazines were stacked neatly in one corner. The second from the top was a recent issue of *Playboy*. He riffled through it until he got to the centerspread. It made him horny. And five thousand miles away on a ship with nothing but five thousand men, he didn't need that. He set it back on the stack, finally settling for a copy of *Mechanix Illustrated*. Much easier on the groin.

Halfway through the rest of the stack, he looked at his watch. It was nearly four. What was keeping Simon?

He dug into his shirt pocket for a cigarette. The pack was empty. He checked around the desks. Nothing. He searched in the drawers. Damn! He ducked his head out the door. There was no one in sight. Couldn't even bum a butt.

Then he remembered a spare pack of Gruber's he'd noticed on the desk when he left the stateroom earlier. It would take him only three or four minutes to get down and back. He looked back guiltily at the phone. If he hurried, though, he'd be back before it stopped ringing. He sprinted off toward the ladder to the third deck.

He left the stateroom door open, and tiptoed quickly over to the desk. Gruber and Lowell were sleeping soundly. Lucky bastards! They not only could sleep, they had comfortable bunks to do it in.

He was about to leave when something assaulted his nostrils, a faint smell compounded of urine and feces. Victor sniffed about. It was coming from the direction of the bunks. He crept over to where Gruber lay. The reek grew stronger.

Then, what he saw made the vomit rise in his gorge.

Half obscured in shadow, Gruber's face was a hideous mask of death. His lifeless eyes bulged unseeing at the bunk above him. His tongue, no longer red, jutted black from between twisted lips. In his death throes or shortly after, he had voided.

Fighting back his rebellious stomach, Victor climbed up and looked into the upper bunk. Lowell's face was as peaceful as a sleeping cherub's, its childlike beauty marred only be a large, ugly patch of dark red in his blond hair where the left side of the skull was stove in. The belt which had also strangled Gruber lay loosely about his throat.

Victor stepped down and tried to collect his thoughts amidst this double nightmare. He bent over and inspected Gruber more closely. He must've put up a furious fight; there were dark bruises and contusions all over his face, and his right arm was bloody where the sleeve was torn just below the elbow.

As he stood bent over the bunk, a sound behind him intruded itself through the normal background noises of the ship. Victor looked around.

Framed in the bright glare of the doorway stood Arnold Gelman. He was leveling a Colt .45 automatic right at the middle of Victor's back.

Simon Roschestvensky stood in the corridor behind him.

FORTY-SEVEN

THE COLD water brought him to. Through a red haze of blood, Kolnikov could just barely define Gelman standing over him, bathed in the harsh glare of the overhead light. Roschestvensky was crowded close behind to his left. The awful swelling about his face and mouth made his skin want to split. He was numb from the waist down from the pummeling his groin had taken just before he had passed out.

He tried to move. Nothing. Every moveable part of him was trussed tightly into the chair.

Gelman reached an arm out, grabbed his hair, and slammed his head back until Victor was staring straight up into the other's face. His neck felt like it would snap against the cold steel backrail of the chair.

"For the last time, Kolnikov . . . *who sent you?*"

Victor could see better now—and hated Gelman with every cell in his body. More than his body ached, he ached to be free to kill this little runt with his bare hands. He wanted to seize that black, curly hair which never set right under an officer's cap and pound that hawking big Jew nose right back into the face it came from.

It hurt him to speak. He had to keep swallowing his own blood as he tried. "Gelman, you Jew mother-fucker," he rasped, "the

Nazis only made one mistake—*they missed you!*" He spat. The blood-red spittle hit Gelman fair in the face, just above his full mouth. Gelman sprang upright just as his right fist rocketed into Victor's face, snapping his head back. The pain from the neck against the chair broke like a crevass up along the back of the skull. That little runt of a kike is *strong*, thought Victor as his head slowly recovered from the blow. Gelman pulled out a handkerchief and wiped off his face. Victor reopened his eyes.

"I'm going to kill you, Gelman." It hurt his mouth to speak, but the words would not be denied. "I'm going to get out of this. And then, I'm going to kill you—and the rest of your nigger-kike family after you."

Gelman pulled his fist back again. Roschestvensky stopped him. "Enough! We're not getting anywhere. You could kill that dumb *kulak* and he'd be cursing us with his last breath." He looked at his watch. "It's nearly zero-five-hundred. We'll be off Piraeus in an hour. Go back with the others."

"But what about him?" Gelman looked as if he regretted not getting in one more last lick.

"Leave him to me. I'll only be about ten minutes. Now get going!"

Gelman's fist looked almost as swollen as Victor's face felt. He massaged it with his left hand as he made his way out into the corridor, reclosing the door behind him carefully.

Roschestvensky pulled the other chair over near Kolnikov and sat down facing him. He took out a silver cigarette case engraved with the Russian Imperial Eagle and held it up before opening it. "My father's," he announced with evident pride, "the only thing he got out with that he didn't sell." Then he selected two cigarettes, lit them simultaneously, and placed one in Victor's lips. Victor turned his head and spat it out.

"Very well then, Victor. Don't join me." He retrieved the rejected cigarette and stubbed it out. Then, slowly, deliberately, he took several languid puffs.

"You're going to die, Victor. You know that, don't you?" Victor sat motionless. "But before we end our . . . ah . . . association . . . let's say I'm still curious. How did you know about this operation? I mean, who put you onto it? And why you?" Simon paused to shift his gangly legs. "After all, it was my idea alone to spring you, though not for the reasons you thought, obviously. You were to be decoys . . . yes . . . but you were supposed to keep attention focused where you were— or were supposed to be—while Gelman, Horn, and Stoddard brought off the operation over here. So how did this come about? Hmm?" He paused again. Kolnikov kept silent.

"Oh come on, Victor. I told you you're going to die. Your little mission here is a failure. The hunted have the hunters. And nothing can stop us now. So why not be a good fellow. Be a sport and tell me."

Victor managed a painful smile.

"You wouldn't believe me if I told you." Victor's mind was fully awake again; it raced to find words, ideas. He gazed away from Roschestvensky. "And besides, your operation is already blown—our being here proves it. There are nuclear weapons experts already on their way. And *Enterprise* and *Nimitz* are *not* proceeding at twenty-five knots cruising speed—they're going *flat out* ... *flank* ... that's fifty knots, Simon. That'll put them here by tomorrow night." Victor glanced over to see what affect his words had. Roschestvensky looked a bit surprised, but not in the least ruffled.

"Still too late, Victor. Because those nukes up topside aren't duds."

Kolnikov jerked his head around and frowned.

"That's right, Victor. Every one of them is alive—and armed." He stopped to chain-light another cigarette, then sat back comfortably, apparently pleased with what was to come next. "You don't play chess, do you? I thought not. Nevertheless, your scenerio involving the duds was ingenious—for a peasant, of course."

Victor's face stayed passive; he wasn't being goaded.

"But mine is better. It has ... let us say ... the quality of breathtaking ruthlessness ... an utter, God-like amorality ... a scope which separates the aristocratic mind from those below it. Such as you.

"You're bright, Victor. Even ruthless. But you have very severe limits. Bounds beyond which your mind can't even begin to travel. So your plan was clever. Brilliant, even. But still, it stops at half measures because you can't imagine a full measure."

"No, Victor. Every one of those nukes is very much alive." He checked his watch. "We arrive off Piraeus in less than an hour, or rather *Forrestal* does—Gelman and I are leaving on the first shuttle flight at zero-five-forty. A car is already waiting for us at the airport. And we'll be safely across the mountains north of Athens—and safely upwind, I might add—half way to Salonika when the great American supercarrier U.S.S. *Forrestal* goes up in the greatest nuclear disaster of all time."

Kolnikov struggled against his bonds. "But that'll be war—all-out nuclear war!"

"No, Victor. It'll be an accident. A most regrettable accident. Between the explosion, the tidal waves, and the fallout—from *your* nuclear accident—Greece and Turkey will virtually cease to exist as nations. Fifty percent of the population of Greece, in fact, are in the Athens area. I suppose you know that. Then, naturally, our forces will move in to restore order."

"You can't! *Enterprise* and *Nimitz* 'll chew you up and spit you all over the nearest Turkish rug."

Roschestvensky leaned over almost to Kolnikov's face.

"*Enterprise* and *Nimitz* won't be permitted through the Straits of Gibraltar!" Simon waved his hands up in a sweeping, explosive motion. "What? Risk a second disaster like that? Or a third? No, Victor. American sea power will be *finished* in the Mediterranean. You won't be permitted back into Naples—Gibraltar, Yokosuka, Subic, *anywhere!*

"And do you think your so-called NATO allies will permit your nuclear forces on their soil? No!" He stood up triumphantly. "America, Victor, will be driven back on her own shores. And without friends or bases anywhere, you'll be forced to capitulate or be destroyed, because you'll be encircled like a tubercular bacillus. We'll have the Middle East in thirty days, with the rest of the world shunning the United States for what she let happen here.

"We won't give up, Victor."

Roschestvensky chuckled. "They'll probably elect Jane Fonda President and appoint Ramsey Clark to head up the surrender delegation."

Kolnikov looked up at Roschestvensky. Try as he might, he couldn't hide the foreboding in his eyes.

"But why, Simon? And why the cradle of Western civilization?"

"Why? To get this stalemate resolved in a way that *will* forestall the inevitable world-destroying clash which *will* come one day if this chess game goes on much longer. That's why!

"As for your so-called Western civilization." He sniffed contemptuously. "Western civilization died in 1914. All we've been doing since is trying to bury the pieces!"

"Why 1914, Simon?"

Roschestvensky shook his head. "You really are still a *kulak*, Victor. You still think

Western civilization was something great, something to look up to. But what is it, really? What was Athens? A bunch of half-queer pointy-heads running a nation of slaves with their hired bully boys! Rome? All queer! And sadists, to boot! The slavery was the same, only on a bigger scale. Christian Europe? Two thousand years of robbery, rapine, war, famine, pillage, and oppression —all to keep whoever got to be king of the hill on top and fat. The nobility? The aristocracy? The chief murderers—the fittest survivors. Not by brains, but by terror and taxation. And what do you stupid peasants do? You glorify it!" He paused for breath, his face a mask of red hatred. "And the Industrial Revolution? Let me tell you . . . that was the biggest of them all! Children in a boyar's dacha never labored so hard as in the mines of Wales and the looms of Worcester. But then they went too far." Simon's eyes began to glitter. "They tried to grab everything—and bumbling, they led their trusting minions into the most massive slaughter in history— into the carnage of the trenches! And they didn't stop even then until, not just Russia, but all of Europe started to revolt. Even then, they didn't quit. They patched things up for awhile, then went at it again, and again . . . and fucking again!

"Victor. Do you know that more people have died violently in the twentieth century than in all the centuries of Mankind's history before that *put together?*" He had been waving his arms; now he dropped them to his sides. "And it has to stop."

"By killing more people and imposing a worldwide dictatorship." Kolnikov smiled. It unsettled Simon's face. "You're crazy, Simon. You're one of those people on the top yourself. How did you, an aristocrat like you, come around to thinking like this?"

"I didn't come around. I was 'recruited,' so to speak—by my father. He saw the rottenness of our class. He *should* have; he was a high operative in the Czarist secret police! After he got to America, he joined the Reds. He wanted world peace and worked for it. He set up the whole organization from the top—where his social position permitted him to move and know people. And he died a General in the KGB."

"And what are you, Simon?"

"I am—or will be—an Admiral in Soviet Naval Intelligence."

"No you're not, Simon. You're an ass—an overbred ass!"

Roschestvensky ignored Victor's insult. He picked up a long length of torn bedsheet and, forcing it into Victor's mouth, tied it around the back of a verticle pipe. Victor could neither talk nor move his head.

"Sorry I can't stay to convert you, Victor, but I must be on my way. But don't feel badly. You came very close."

As he reached the door, he halted, hesitated, and looked back at Victor with an expression that bordered on regret.

"Actually, Victor. I'm sorry to lose you. Really I am."

And he locked the door with the key he had picked up from the desk.

FORTY-EIGHT

VICTOR TESTED his hands. No use. They had been done by professionals. The pipe behind his head was cutting into the back of his skull. Waves of pain were constantly growing out from the epicenter, up into his head and down his spine and into his shoulders. But to press forward was to cut off the minuscule air passage the gag left him.

He sat back in the near-total darkness, trying to make his body at least as easy as possible. The same couldn't be said for his mind.

What time was it? Without even ship's bells—which wouldn't begin until reveille at 0600—he could only guess. Gruber—or Gruber's body, rather—wasn't helping. It kept belching and farting at irregular intervals as the organs began their process of decomposition. Once, when Gelman was working over his groin, Victor had vomited, and that too contributed to the general reek of the place.

Only poor Lowell—ever the New England gentleman—seemed to be minding his manners. But for how long?

How long? Victor could feel the tides of panic rising now. Besides twenty million Greeks and Turks and several thousand Americans, he had his own skin to think of. Until day before yesterday, the only fireball he had contemplated was the sun over Ipenema Beach.

What was the time of ignition? Let's see. What did Simon say? The plane at 0540. That would put him at the airport about 0600. Salonika was about two hundred kilometers. Three to four hours. But only an hour—give or take—to get them over to the other side of the mountains where they'd be shielded from both the blast and most of the heat. Christ, what a fireball it was going to be—a hundred-odd nukes! Going to be? Shit!

Back to probable time of ignition. He had to give himself an hour, at least. Christ! He forgot about Black! Oh, God! True to type, he had meticulously moved the gear he'd need over to . . . whatsisname? Schermerhorn. Schermerhorn's stateroom. Damn!

But what about breakfast? No. Probably not before 0700. 0700! That's the probable time of ignition! Even if they come by early—even a quarter hour—was there time? Horn and Stoddard could hold them off. Horn and Stoddard! Simon did say only him and Gelman. Probably couldn't get everybody off without raising suspicion, so they're getting the top guys off. Maybe they'd come early with breakfast? Doors locked, and Simon took the key!

Just then, somebody tried the locked door. Victor wrenched around violently in the chair. Not enough noise to be heard over the sounds of the ship. Then, he heard a jangle of keys, followed by one being slipped into the lock. The door was opened carefully.

Standing in the doorway, a long chain

connecting the open door with his belt like a shiny metal umbilical cord, was Mike Schermerhorn!

He stood a moment, letting his eyes adjust to the dark, then exclaimed, "Jesus fucking Christ on a crutch! What happened to you?" he continued as he crossed the room. He paused a moment to let his mind catch up with his eyes. Kolnikov begged him with his eyes to hurry up setting him free. Schermerhorn got the message. Digging into his pocket, he fished up a long penknife, dug out a blade, and cut away Victor's gag.

"What happened to you, Commander?" demanded the puzzled redhead. "Christ! It stinks like a shithouse in here!"

"I'll explain in a minute. Cut the rest of these straps—quick! The other two are dead." He cocked his head toward the bunks.

Schermerhorn had Victor free in under a minute. Then he helped the big man onto his very unsteady feet. Mike whistled as he surveyed the damage to Kolnikov's face. "Who worked *you* over—Michael Spinks?"

Victor steadied himself against the stateroom sink. "Turn on the lights, Mike. I'll tell you as we go. We haven't much time."

"Aye-aye, sir." A switch clicked, and a flood of light bathed the room in an antiseptic blue-white aura. Antiseptic was more than Victor could say for his face. One eye was completely closed; his mouth looked like what the pet-food commercials call "beef by-product." He ran the cold water and splashed it generously over his savaged skin. At least now his face felt better than his groin. He wished he had time to soak that too. He took off his coat and tie. Then he splashed his face some more, patting it dry ever so gently with a hand towel.

Then he turned to Schermerhorn as he prepared to leave the room.

"Mike. Here's the scoop. And it's straight! Some people are onboard this ship and are planning to blow the whole fucking thing sky high in a little more than an hour unless I can stop them!"

"Are you serious, Commander?"

"Are they?" Victor pointed first to his face, then to the dead men.

"What can I do?"

"What time is it, Mike?"

"Sir, it's . . . zero-five-hundred."

"Good! Okay . . . here's one thing you can do. There's a shuttle plane due to take off at zero-five-forty, if not before. STOP THAT FLIGHT. In fact, have ALL flights stopped."

"Me, sir?"

"Yes, you. Tell the Captain or Exec or anybody else you can find what's happened here. And then—lay down on the Flight Deck if you have to—but don't let anything off. Is that clear?"

"Yes, *sir!*"

Kolnikov hobbled painfully out of the door. He staggered.

"Can I help you, Commander?"

"No. I can make it. You just go do what I told you—on the double."

Schermerhorn zipped up his nylon jacket before going. A thought suddenly occurred to him.

"Y'know, Commander, I had just come over to see what you people wanted for breakfast. Lucky I remembered, huh?"

"Yes it was. And thank you."

FORTY-NINE

To THOSE who harbor visions of the Gates of Hell, the entrance to the W Spaces aboard *Forrestal* must come as a disappointment.

It's quite simply a plain corridor running aft for about thirty feet from a thwartships passageway on the Second Deck. Sandwiched between the ship's administrative offices, it could easily be missed by the casual passerby —unless he chanced to turn into it.

The corridor deadends at a bulkhead the upper half of which is painted white—not green like the rest. Large letters, painted on in red, read:

HALT! W DIVISION *HALT!*
PROHIBITED AREA
DO NOT CROSS RED LINE
WITHOUT AUTHORIZATION

A Marine sentry stands in front of the sign, a submachine gun at the ready. It is loaded and cocked. Below the peephole on the door to his left is a bank of ID photographs, with the names of the fewer than four dozen persons permitted to enter that door—the Captain, the Exec, the Admiral, and W Division Officer, and the officers and men who work for him. Everyone must be sight-checked and cleared individually every time by the sentry.

A white line is painted on the deck across the mouth of the corridor; two paces in, a yellow line; two paces beyond, a red line. The instant *anyone* steps into the corridor, the sentry slips the safety to "off" and challenges. The intruder must stop at the yellow line, identify himself, show a special ID card, and have his photo verified against its mate on the door before he dares take a step further.

The sentry has one categorical order: shoot to kill anyone who steps past the red line without permission. In the twenty feet between the red line and where he stands, the sentry can—and will—cut a man in half with a flaming scythe of high-velocity .45-caliber bullets before he could make it half way.

Victor had started out, then thought better of essaying entry into the W Spaces in just his blood-spattered shirt. So he had gone back and put on tie and jacket, tilting the brim of his cap as far down over his battered face as he dared.

He passed the Disbursing Office on his way, and regretted being so hasty in returning Black's .45. But then, that would mean killing the guard as—even with the drop on him—the Marine wouldn't give up. It had to be done differently.

Trying his best to overcome the crippling pain between his legs, Victor first walked past the entrance to the W Corridor—better known as Machinegun Alley—at a normal pace.

The sentry was alone, but very much on alert, as usual.

He stopped as soon as he got out of sight on the other side, mainly to compose his thoughts.

There'd be no bluffing his way into this one. And trying would only find him staring down the business end of the barrel, with the safety off and a ruthlessly determined finger on the trigger. Damned Gung-Ho Jar Heads!

And no end runs. It'd have to be straight down the middle with all you've got, Victor. Hit him fast, low, and hard. There'd be no second down.

Victor studied the opening. A coaming ran up each side. Good! He could grab onto the near one as he made his turn . . . keep him from skidding and increase his speed—sort of playing Crack-the-Whip.

Victor took several more steps further down the passage, and leaned against the bulkhead. He took a deep breath. And now he was suddenly aware that he was terribly afraid. The blood coursing from his pounding heart made every capillary in his head and face feel like an overloaded storm sewer.

He took one last look in each direction. No one coming. One more deep breath. Crouch over low . . . and GO-O-O-O!

Grasping the lip of the coaming as he rounded into the corridor, Victor charged across the deadly ten yards at the startled sentry like the prize center he had once been —head lowered, left arm up to fend off the fatal barrel. His head crashed into the guard's middle, propelling him like a tackling dummy into the bulkhead behind, where they both dropped in a heap. The gun flew against the left bulkhead and onto the deck with a raucous clatter. Victor dove for it and, scrambling up on his feet, cradled the butt in the crook of his arm.

The sentry was out cold. Victor tried the door; it was locked. But the pounding of footsteps on the ladder inside told him he was no longer unexpected. He leveled the gun at the door. The peephole opened and a voice called through to the outside. Victor squeezed the trigger.

Nothing. He had hit that poor kid so fast, he hadn't got the safety off! Victor flipped the catch and squeezed again. A stream of bullets stitched a line of lethal black holes diagonally across the door. Agonized screams, followed by the thump-clump of falling bodies confirmed that he'd hit more than merely sheet metal. He braced the gun firmly and let fly another, longer burst at the handle and lock. The door swung slightly ajar and stopped. Victor charged it shoulder first; the body wedged against it flopped to the other side of the landing, its lifeless face lolling wide-eyed up at him. Stoddard. He stepped onto the top of the ladder. Horn lay half way down it, tangled grotesquely backwards across a handrail.

Now with the bone of blood hatred in his teeth, Victor leaped over Horn's body. But as his feet hit the deck, his right ankle twisted under him. An excruciating shaft of pain shot up his leg, joining and doubling the pain in his groin and sending him crashing heavily to the hard deck. As he struggled up on one knee, a bullet whizzed over his head and ricocheted around behind him. Kolnikov recovered his gun and fired a burst in the direction from which it had come—just in time to see Roschestvensky duck behind a desk, .45 in hand. Gelman was standing ten feet away, unarmed and cowering in the middle of the room. Victor swung his gun toward him. Gelman spun away to the right and behind a file cabinet as the lethal spray sought him. Victor saw at least one shot strike his left arm above the elbow, spattering the bulkhead beyond with blood and shards of blasted flesh.

Staying in his low crouch, Victor swung around in search of Roschestvensky. He instinctively shifted location just as Simon emerged firing from his hiding place. Simon's second bullet narrowly missed him, tearing up padding as it bore through the shoulder of his jacket. Kolnikov pulled the trigger to fire back. Nothing happened. Empty! And the spare clip was on the Marine's belt topside!

Roschestvensky stood up for a better aim. Victor threw the heavy machinegun at him. It struck him full in the chest, sending his next shot wild.

Disarmed, and with Gelman and Roschestvensky alive and kicking, Victor opted for a second round at a later time.

Ignoring the agony in his ankle, he sprang up the ladder before Simon could regain his bearings.

The kid was still out cold when Victor half-ran, half-hobbled through the door back into Machinegun Alley.

Where now? The Bridge? The OD's pistol! It was his only chance. As he turned into the passageway, the sound of running footsteps behind him said, "Move Out!"

Animal fear is stronger than pain. It propelled Victor to the bottom landing of the escalator to the Flight Deck nearly as fast as two perfectly good feet might have. He stopped to consider its narrow, five-deck length. Christ! It looked like Mount Everest— and no fucking cover! Then fear regained the upper hand.

He was nearly at the top when a loud report, followed by the twang of dancing metal, announced Simon's arrival at the bottom of the long, slanting shaft. Victor drew on the dregs of terror for the last half-deck dash to the upper landing.

But once up—what? He couldn't outdistance Simon up four more switchback ladders to the Bridge.

Victor hopped out through the inboard hatch onto the Flight Deck, his eyes desperately searching for *something—anything!* The nearest person was the Marine guard posted behind the first Phantom of the starboard catapult.

His rifle!

Victor galloped over and grabbed it. The amazed Marine wrenched back on it. "What's the matter, Commander?" he shouted. "You crazy, sir? This area is restricted, you can't . . ." As the force of their struggle wheeled him around Victor, a shot from Simon's .45 halted his sentence in midword. He slumped away onto the deck.

Ignoring the gun that fell with him, Victor ducked under the Phantom's after stabilator. With the plane's fuselage temporarily shielding him from his fast-closing pursuer, he skipped forward and up onto the low, broad wing, seeking cover wherever it could be found.

Simon rounded the tail just as Victor was struggling over the lip of the open cockpit. He raised his gun. Too late. Victor wriggled across and out the other side, crouching low on the starboard wing.

The sun was full up, and everything—and everybody—stood out vividly in the brilliant Aegean morning.

He heard Simon's feet clambering up onto the opposite wing. Then he took his chance.

With one final, pain-defying effort, he pushed away from the fuselage, ran out along the trailing edge of the wing as far as possible, and vaulted for the deck. But his bad ankle betrayed him. A loud snap, followed by a flash of agony that turned the world bright red, told him he hadn't made it.

He rolled on his back, stifling a groan.

Simon was leaning across the cockpit, aiming. Victor rolled again and a bullet chewed up the rubber non-skid on the deck in the middle of where he had just been.

Victor spun back and tried to crawl. The catwalk! Only feet away!

His right leg was totally useless. Struggling up on his arms, he pushed forward frantically with his good leg. If he could reach the edge, he could pull himself over into sanctuary, at least for the moment. He twisted his head to see behind him.

Simon was standing on the near side of the cockpit—half in, half out. He sat down on the lip and braced his back against the canopy. And took careful aim.

Victor stretched out on his face and tried to time his next roll. His arm was already half over the edge of the deck, but he had neither the strength nor time to pull himself over.

And then he felt it! The catapult safety handle! He yanked it to the left and, fumbling lower down, stabbed the firing button home.

Roschestvensky's startled yelp blended with the crack of his final shot as the great bird squatted down on its perch. The slug missed by a cunt hair. Victor turned his head and watched, mesmerized, as the plane— first in seeming slow motion, then faster and faster—rocketed down the deck, its mounting G-forces pinning Roschestvensky to the back of the cockpit in a curiously obscene embrace.

He saw the steel yoke snap the Phantom into the air at more than a hundred fifty knots—strangely silent without the usual infernal roar of her powerful jets.

Yet even without them, she tried to gain altitude, soaring ahead of the ship for awhile like some prehistoric seagull. Then she suddenly faltered and, stalling, dipped from sight.

Victor waited the long minutes for what must follow.

When it did, the topmost plumes of spray sparkled gold in the hot Easter sunrise. And seconds later, seventy-six thousand tons of steel passed over Simon Roschestvensky's watery grave like the Judgment of God.

Victor subsided onto his back and surveyed the deep blue sky.

It was Easter. *Christos anesti,* everybody. Doomsday is over! Rejoice! Tears were pouring out and over the sides of his face. *Christos anesti! Alithos anesti!* Yes . . . *Christos . . .*

A curious knot of men were standing over him. Among them was Arnold Gelman, his bloodied left sleeve torn up the length of his arm and wrapped in a makeshift tourniquet.

In the other hand, he was holding a .45.

FIFTY

THE FIRST thing Victor saw was his right leg sticking up and out of the white sheets at a forty-five degree angle like some elephantine erection. The second was the armed Marine guard. Victor figured the antiseptic room to be one of the isolation spaces in the ship's Sick Bay.

As soon as he bestirred himself, the Marine lifted the telephone receiver off its cradle near the door and dialed it.

Several minutes later, there was a knock on the door. The Marine unlocked it and admitted Arnold Gelman, preceded by two officers in tropical whites. The taller one's shoulder boards counted four gold stripes on its blue field; the shorter's the solid gold field and two silver stars of a Rear Admiral. Each wore gold wings above a massive block of ribbons. The tall one reached down and grasped Victor's right hand in a firm, masculine grip.

"Commander Kolnikov, I understand that you're to be congratulated." Victor's eyes darted from the Captain to Gelman, who had moved up along the other side of the bed. "That's all right," the Captain continued in a reassuring baritone. "Commander Hartranft . . . er, *Gelman* here's told us about you . . . how you saved my ship and all of us from disaster—and worse. Oh . . . incidentally, I'm Captain Means, and this is Admiral Mark,

Commander, Carrier Division Four." He relinquished his hold on Victor's hand to the Admiral.

The Admiral added his accolades.

"I was just walking onto the Flag Bridge this morning when I heard the commotion on the Flight Deck and caught the last bit of action between you and that Captain . . . what's his name?"

"Roschestvensky," volunteered Gelman.

"Roschestvensky, yes. And that was just about the fastest piece of thinking on anyone's part I've ever seen. Congratulations, Commander—you're a hero."

Kolnikov, covered the questions bombarding his head with a noncommital smile. "Did you see him hit, Admiral?"

"Just barely, before the whole thing disappeared under the bow." Victor gave an involuntary shudder. The Admiral read his thoughts and waved his hand deprecatingly. "Don't worry. From that height at the speed he was traveling, he didn't know what hit him. There weren't enough pieces left big enough for the screws to chew up."

Now it was the Captain's turn to shudder. "I hope the weapon's still in one piece."

"I told you, John," the Admiral insisted, "I saw it break away and go in the drink about fifty yards ahead of the point of impact."

"Let's hope that was it," he rejoindered, his ruddy, hawklike face registering seesawing hope and concern. He turned to Kolnikov and shook his hand once more. "Now you'll have to excuse us while we find our little toy on the bottom of the Aegean before the shit hits the fan the way it did in Spain back in Sixty-seven. Congratulations again . . . and . . . thanks."

Gelman saw them out, then ordered the guard to wait outside. As he headed back to Victor's bed, he drew up a chair and sat down.

"Well, Victor . . . you heard them—you're a hero, even at the cost of dropping a live nuke in an ally's territorial waters and fucking up my operation."

"Your operation?" Victor's head was starting to whirl.

"Yes. You killed the number-two mole—Roschestvensky."

"The number-*two* mole?" The whirl was now a merry-go-round.

"Number-two . . . or three . . . or four. We don't know, or rather, we're not completely certain."

Victor had managed to put the brakes on his thoughts. His eyes bore in questioningly on Gelman's.

"Okay, Gelman. Enlighten me." He searched around the room. "But first, can you find me a smoke somewhere around here . . . or better yet . . . a smoke *and* a drink?"

Gelman got up, opened the door a crack, and said something to the sentry. "Tell him to make it a double . . . no, a triple!" Victor shouted after him. Gelman nodded, closed the door, and walked back, collecting a pack of cigarettes and a lighter from atop a nearby instrument stand. He handed the cigarette to Kolnikov and flicked on the lighter. The Marine returned with a large tumbler of clear, brown liquid before Victor even had the cigarette going properly. Victor tasted it. Issue brandy, but passable.

Both sat silently while Victor savored enough of both cigarette and brandy. Finally, Kolnikov lowered the partially emptied glass to his lap, took one final deep drag, let it out slowly, and spoke to Gelman.

"Okay. *Now* enlighten me."

Gelman turned his face upward at the overhead light and grimaced, obviously framing his next words carefully.

"Let's go back to square one, Victor." He looked unblinking at him now. "Simon was the head mole of this whole operation. It was his idea, or most of it was. And he was the one who framed you and Gruber and Lowell—you were getting too close to us. It was also his idea to spring you three as a diversion—to keep Washington looking the wrong way while we pulled off the big hit over here. But, as you know, it backfired . . . on all of us, in fact."

"All of *who?*"

"Our side." Victor gave a start; Gelman smiled. "You see, Victor, Simon was the number-two mole—or three or four, as I said—and I'm . . . or I was . . . the number-one counter-mole. I've been trying for fourteen years to discover—or rather, prove—who controls him. And on up the line. That's why I rode this thing all the way down the wire—hoping that, when it misfired, the foxes up top would break cover; or that Roschestvensky would panic and do something to blow their cover. But by bringing him over here and then killing him you severed the main link." Gelman heaved a long sigh. He looked tired, and a little exasperated. "Now we have to shift gears, and hope somehow that Simon's death and the shortcircuiting of their grand design will shake something—or somebody loose."

Victor felt a little crestfallen. He took another long sip of his drink. He pondered awhile before speaking.

"But weren't you taking an awful risk? I mean, going this far?"

Gelman dismissed the question with his hand. "We had to—there was no other way. Besides, we had everything covered. Our own nuclear weapons officers standing by onboard to replace Horn and Stoddard—and me. It would've never gone down."

"But what about all those Russians at the border now? What if they decide to go in anyway?"

Gelman's eyes glittered. "I hope they do, Victor. I really hope they do."

"You *hope?*"

"Yes, I hope. God, do I hope! Because we're ready for them, this time. And not with the *Forrestal.*" A gleefully malevolent smirk took possession of Gelman's dark face as he explained. "Victor . . . every one of the roads on every one of the mountain valleys they'll have to pass through have been mined—tactical neutron weapons set to sweep every valley like a sawed-off shotgun, and other nukes set deep to turn every exit—every pass, every defile—into an avalanche of radioactive rubble. We've already pulled out the civilian populace. When we get done with them—*if* they come through—they'll look like Roschestvensky after the *Forrestal* ran over him! Between thirty and forty Soviet and satellite divisions will be annihilated—wiped out!" Gelman clapped his hands. "And what's left of them the Greeks and Turks'll mop up— that should be another fun show, especially with the Turks."

"Well, it looks as if I've fucked things up royally."

"Not really, Victor. There's a total communications blackout on this task group, at the moment—partly to keep the lid on so we can, hopefully, retrieve that nuke before word gets out—it's very shallow right here— and secondly, to keep Simon's keepers jittery. They don't know whether he's alive or dead—or worse, a counter-mole himself. We're picking up everybody in the entire operation right this minute."

"That must be a big haul just in itself."

"More than a hundred people—in just about every place you can imagine." He gestured at Victor. "You know what it took. Just to set the three of us up here. The FBI checks. The complete histories—every place they had to be. The orders to get us transferred here. And we've got them all, the biggest cleanup in history. And we're watching the rest; anyone who bolts now is literally a marked man."

"Well, I'm sorry if I screwed up anything." Victor finished his drink. Gelman took his glass and, going over to the door, passed it out to the Marine with instructions for a refill. He waited until it arrived, then brought it back to Victor.

"And I'm sorry I had to work you over like I did. Nothing personal, you understand."

Victor nodded, though ruefully.

"Who killed Gruber and Lowell?"

"Roschestvensky. With Horn and Stoddard. And he would've killed you too, except that he was frantic to know how you got here. Or rather, who sent you." Gelman suddenly paused and looked up. "Who did send you? Or can't you say?"

"I can't say." Victor's heart had leaped at Gelman's question. He was grateful for the excuse not to answer. He shifted the focus of the conversation.

"Did you say you were after Simon for fourteen years?"

"Yes. And after the ring for years before that. You see, I was a super double mole. I was recruited before I even went to college— by my father."

"Simon said his father recruited him."

"Yes, he was a KGB agent. We knew that years ago."

"We?"

"They, actually. My father was an agent for Israeli Intelligence ostensibly working for the KGB. I was recruited and doubled before my freshman year at NYU. Later on, I was maneuvered into Naval Intelligence under Roschestvensky, though it took three years of very careful cultivation before he picked up on me.

"So you see, Victor . . . you might say I've

been after him more than half my life."

Kolnikov regarded Gelman searchingly. "Israeli Intelligence—Mossad—KGB, ONI . . . do you *really* know who you're working for?"

Gelman pulled a wry face. "Do any of us?"

Kolnikov hung his head and shook it back and forth slowly. Then he looked up.

"You know, Gelman, I've not only misjudged you, I've hated you. Hated your guts for as long as I've known you."

Gelman made a gesture distilled from millennia of oppression.

"Nhu? So who doesn't?"

He only half smiled.

FIFTY-ONE

THE OFFICERS' Motor Boat nosed confidently through the muck of the Inner Harbor, nudging itself smartly against the Navy pier.

Gelman scrambled easily up onto the landing and, turning, helped Kolnikov up with the aid of the after boatswain. As they neared the main gate, they heard newsboys hawking papers featuring renewed disturbances along the Sino-Soviet border. Deprived of their nuclear Trojan Horse, the Soviets had set up shop in a safer place.

"Looks like our friends chickened out," observed Kolnikov.

"More likely some sonofabitch tipped them to our booby traps," rejoined Gelman. "We'll get him too."

"I'm sure you will, Arnold. I gather from what little you've said that some of the bigger moles ran out into your traps."

"Quite a few. Including some we didn't expect—and so high up it'll be too embarrassing to blow them publically."

"So what do we do then?"

"They get to spill their guts—all their guts—and retire quietly. Or they meet with an accident."

"Fair enough—I guess."

When Kolnikov reached the gate, he stopped and took Gelman's hand.

"Thank you, Arnold. Especially for

clearing me with Washington."

Gelman grew grim. "You know they won't be able to vindicate you publically—also too embarrassing. But, I do wish you'd reconsider about staying in." He shifted feet like an awkward youth. "Except for the disarming of the nukes, your analysis was uncanny. And after nine years out of it . . . didn't mean to touch a sore spot . . . we need people with your ability."

Kolnikov set his jaw.

"No way. It's already cost too much. Nine years. Gruber. Lowell." He paused. "And . . . a man I thought was my friend for nearly twenty years." He straightened up. "No, Arnold. I'm going to do my best to forget this dirty business. And do some normal living. I've got three of us to do it for now."

"Well, don't forget they want you back in Washington for debriefing in two weeks."

"I won't."

"Also, I wish you would stay here—up at the hospital at COMSOUTH—instead of going off to Rome."

"Uh-uh. I'm going to have a date with a beautiful woman."

"In that condition?"

"Even if I have to rent a stand-in."

Victor turned toward the Piazza. Gelman touched his arm.

"I do still have one more question. I know you said you can't talk about it, but . . . I'm dying to know just how you did it."

Victor gave him a smile and a parting wave.

"Arnold . . . you wouldn't believe me if I told you."

FIFTY-TWO

JUST OUTSIDE the gate, Victor nearly collided with Lieutenant JG Black running to make the boat back.

"Oh, excuse me, Commander," he blurted out breathless. "Are you leaving?" As it was obvious that Victor was, he stuck out his hand. "Well, sir. It was a pleasure knowing you . . . or sort of . . . or, well, you know what I mean. Anyway, goodbye and good luck." He stole a glance at the waiting boat. "And you did square away the mess bill for yourself and the other two gentlemen with Mister Schermerhorn?" (How typical of the Supply breed, thought Kolnikov—go on his ship to rob it, then save it, and he can still think about a mess bill!)

"Yes, I did, son—wouldn't want to cheat you."

Black thought that one over for a second or two and then excused himself, but, before finally heading down the pier, he added, "It's a good thing you came when you did. Two weeks later, and you'd've run into the *real* audit team. Just got a message they're waiting out on the ship . . . that's why I'm rushing."

He threw Kolnikov a salute on the run, and jumped into the boat just as it started to drift clear of the dock.

FIFTY-THREE

VICTOR MADE his way as rapidly as his crutches would let him up Piazza Municipio past the somber Castel Nouvo, where the usurper Charles of Durazzo had ordered Queen Joanna of Naples strangled and her corpse exposed for six days in the Cathedral before burying her just to consolidate his succession.

A little way up, another car occupied the place formerly filled by his rented one. The "official" *guardia* had no recall of such an automobile having been there.

At the rental office, the girl explained that it had been returned to them—for a price, of course.

"But they're very good about it," she explained. "Sometimes they even wash them."

Back at the Hotel Londra, Victor telephoned New York. Then he took a taxi to the railroad station—but not before checking to see whether or not the driver had been running the meter *before* he got in.

FIFTY-FOUR

Commander Victor Joseph Kolnikov, USN, sipped his third *aperitivo* with the air of a man who has the Establishment by the ass and knows it. He could have opted for one of the fashionable tourists cafes on the Via Veneto, but chose instead a comfortable hole-out-of-the-wall on Piazza del Popolo, where the Roman sun was just as warming, the crowd much thinner, and the prices much more reasonable.

He wasn't really a full Commander—not yet, anyway. He had just taken Gelman's suggestion that he replace the Supply Corps oak leaves with a proper Line star a step further —just so Washington got the picture. He intended to retire as a Commander *at the minimum* and, preferably, as a Captain. After all, Roschestvensky, his classmate—and traitor, spy, saboteur—had made Captain in Kolnikov's enforced absence, so why not Kolnikov himself?

Active duty now was out of the question. Nine years was too long to pick up the tangled skein of Intelligence. Too much had happened; too much would have changed. Trying to go back now would make him appear like the Gung Ho alumnus at Home-coming Weekend. And he wasn't going to be suffered like one of them.

No. He would settle for a comfortable

retirement. Nine years' back pay would come to a tidy sum; added to a Commander's or Captain's pension, that'd make a good base, even in inflation-wracked Italy.

And then there was Tina.

Kolnikov looked at his watch. Only two more hours before he had to get into gear to meet the plane from New York.

Tina could take up decorating for rich Americans in Rome. Certainly she had the contacts—and the goods on enough of them that she wouldn't even have to ask for their business. It would find her—out of guilt or fear or, perhaps, even gratitude. Victor wouldn't be a multimillionaire as planned, but when both of them got done cashing in their chits, life would be pleasant indeed. And free as well.

Yes. Rome was going to be home base for both of them . . . at the expense of the U.S. Navy and of those who rest their sumptuous life styles on a base of working people.

The thought was as warming as the sun itself.

His reverie was intruded upon by the hawking of a newspaper vendor. Something caught Kolnikov's eye, something that piqued his curiosity . . . a headline.

The *Rome Daily American* was proclaiming "WORLD'S BIGGEST HEIST" in huge, red banners.

Victor bought a copy . . . devoured the rest of the story in a glance:

"Six million dollars . . . missing from the U.S.S. *Forrestal* . . . ship's Disbursing Officer sought . . . last seen departing ship with financial inspection team from Washington . . . etc., etc., etc. . . .''

Victor Kolnikov started to laugh. And once started, he couldn't stop. The strapping on his ribs hurt him. It didn't matter.

He couldn't control himself. He guffawed out loud, his booming voice unsettling the early morning coffee drinkers seated nearby. They watched him, puzzled. Great tears were pouring down over the bruised-black face, tears he bothered neither to hide nor wipe.

Then he fished a ten-thousand-lire note out of his wallet—too much by thousands for the bill, even with tip—and tossed it on the table beside him. Then, struggling up on his casted leg and hurriedly adjusting his crutches under his shoulders, he hobbled off after the newspaper vendor. He was still laughing just as hard when he pressed another ten-thousand-lire note into the incredulous vendor's hand.

Then turning back, he made his way eastward toward Piazza di Spagna, his mirth echoing progressively further away down the Via del Babuino.

The Italians who had shared the scene of Kolnikov's sudden eruption crowded around the abandoned paper while one of their number interpreted.

"*Pazza americano,*" one of them muttered, shrugging Latin-style. "Crazy American!"